LETTING GO

A RAINIER FAMILY NOVEL

ASHTON CADE

GRANT

"Save me!" Scout cries, hiding behind me under the big shady oak tree.

"Save you from what?"

She wrinkles her nose, looking over my shoulder like she's worried she's going to be attacked by a bear. But we're not in the wilderness. We're surrounded by the whole town down at the lake for the annual Memorial Day barbecue.

"*Mrs. Giddons,*" she says, her voice almost a hiss.

I frown. "The old lady that owns the inn? Why are you avoiding her?"

Scout rolls her eyes and gives me a sigh and an impatient look. "I know you've been away at college for a few years, but have you already forgotten what a nightmare she is?"

I shrug. "I remember her being... unpleasant."

Scout snorts. "Unpleasant barely *begins* to describe it. Oh, good, I think she's distracted with Barb."

"What does she want with you?"

Scout shakes her head. "I'll tell you about it later. Enjoy the party!" She flits off before I can say anything else and I'm left watching my sister mingle in the crowd instead of doing it myself.

It's weird being back in my hometown as an adult. I feel like most people around here are still looking at me as Sheryl's baby—I know Mom definitely is. It's the whole reason I'm even here this summer: to make my mom happy before her youngest boy goes off to find a real grown-up job in the city.

I really don't see what the big deal is. It's only three hours away. It's not like I won't be able to come back and visit any time. But moms are like that, sometimes, I guess. Especially mine.

So I'm here at this barbeque, feeling awkward because it's the first time I've been to one of these things as my own man, not just as one of Sheryl and Greg's passel of kids.

The whole family's here -- minus the usual absentees -- Aunt Aislynn, Uncle Derick, and their kids, all my cousins. But the barbeque isn't completely overrun by Rainiers. There are people from town, some I recognize, some I don't. There's Mr. Bell, an older man, hunched with is age by now, hanging around under a shady oak, a younger guy next to him. That must be Carson, his grandson. It's been a few years since I've been back to town, but Carson and I were in high school around the same time, so I recognize him. Seems like he never made it out of Umberland.

Then there's old Mrs. Giddons -- the one Scout was avoiding for whatever reason -- and sure enough, she's still talking at Barb, the other woman obviously looking for an escape. I never knew Barb all that well, even when she was married to my cousin Ryan, but now that they're divorced -- and from what I've heard, she was in the wrong -- I don't feel too bad about her predicament.

It's strange how a town like this can stay the same while still changing so much. But as I expected, there isn't anyone

I'm interested in making conversation with. So I'm just minding my own business, eyes roving the crowd for something interesting.

I freeze, eyes landing on over six-feet of solid carved-out-of-marble muscle.

Oh God, I think. *It can't be... can it?* He's perfection, even from this distance. Bigger and broader than I remember. Not the scrawny kid off to try his luck in the majors. I knew he was back in town, but I didn't know he was going to be *here*.

I swallow before remembering the frosty beer in my hand and then I down most of it to cure the dryness in my throat.

Ian Barrett, back in Umberland. What are the odds?

My brother Trevor had mentioned his old friend from high school was coming back to town with plans to restore the old summer camp on the opposite side of the lake. I had no idea it had already happened.

One mention of Ian made my insides turn to jelly, but I'd told myself that it was just the lingering effects on the crush I always had on him. What kid sibling *didn't* have a crush on their older brother's best friend?

Seeing him across the party now brings all those old feelings rushing to the surface, and I can't help but stare at him. I thought I was over him, but clearly I'm not.

And Ian has aged remarkably well. He's always been the older guy, which was attractive in its own right, but now he's filled out from his time in the Major Leagues. He's got a dark dusting of stubble along his square, chiseled jaw, and even from a hundred yards away, I can see the thick veins in his corded forearms.

I go to take another long drink from my beer, but it's empty this time. Not only that, but before I look away from Ian, he glances in my direction, catches my eye, and starts heading *right* for me.

I panic, my heart racing as I watch him approach, completely frozen in place.

"Look at Grant all grown up," he says, smiling as he comes over. I chuckle nervously, taking a nonexistent sip from my empty beer bottle.

"Hey, Ian. Trevor mentioned you were coming back to town."

His smile never falters. "Yeah, I've been back for a couple of months now. He didn't tell me *you* were back. What've you been up to?"

For a minute, I'm hung up on why Trevor would mention me coming back to town to Ian, but then I realize he's still waiting for an answer and I'm standing there like a mute fool.

"I just finished up college," I manage to say. "Mom wanted me back for the summer while I look for a job in the city to start in fall."

"What kind of work are you looking for?"

I shrug. "My degree is in Urban Planning, so I'm hoping to get a job working for the city."

He grins and heat pours through my veins, all the way to my toes. It has nothing to do with the warm May day and everything to do with how his blue-green eyes sparkle at me.

"I meant for the summer."

"Oh… oh!" I feel my face heat to a million degrees and I just want to bury my head in the sand. But Ian's looking at me and he's making me feel squirmy inside with that smile, so I can't run away from him even if it seems to be the only way to save myself from certain embarrassment.

"I don't know. Mom offered me a job at the diner, but I don't really want to cook or serve and there's not a whole lot else for options."

He nods, scratching his chin thoughtfully. I'm acutely

aware of the rest of the party going on around us, but I can't pull my eyes away from Ian. From his broad shoulders filling out the plaid button-down, to the muscles of his forearms, revealed by his pushed-up sleeves, down to his thick callused fingers wrapped around a bottle.

I think about those fingers wrapped around something else and have to bite the inside of my cheek to hold in a moan. Yeah, this little boyhood crush on Ian is *not* dead in any way. If anything, seeing him like this—a solid block of *man*, rather than the lanky athletic boy that left Umberland— only makes the crush worse.

"Do you have any construction experience?" he asks, and I force myself to focus on the conversation at hand, replaying his words in my head to parse the information out of them.

"A little. Trevor let me work for him the summer between high school and college."

He frowns. "I don't remember that."

"You were already gone," I point out, hoping he doesn't hear the hint of bitterness in my voice. It wasn't his fault he left to have a professional baseball career. I certainly can't blame him for following his dreams.

Besides, if Ian had stuck around, I might not have gone to college after all. It may have been a silly crush, but even back then, there was something about the guy that captivated me and made me kind of stupid.

"I guess I was," he says thoughtfully. "Well, I could use some help restoring the old camp and Trevor charges way too damn much." He laughs, and I chuckle too, knowing that's not exactly the case. I'm pretty sure Trevor wouldn't charge Ian a dime if he could avoid it, but the problem isn't will, it's timing. Trevor's booked out months in advance, his construction business booming as our little town experiences a bit of a resurgence.

"You mean it?" I ask, not wanting to get my hopes up in case it's just an offhand comment.

Ian shoots that grin at me again and nods. "Yeah, why the hell not? Would be nice to have some company out there."

"It sounds a lot better than cooking," I say. Not to mention it's an excuse to spend extra time with Ian. Just because nothing's ever going to happen between us doesn't mean there's anything wrong with enjoying a little eye candy, right?

A loud shriek and a big splash calls our attention to the lake and instantly my blood turns to ice. Ian's brow furrows, his forehead wrinkling with a serious look as people start to rush toward the lakeshore. He joins the crowd and I follow on instinct, using Ian's big bulk to hide behind, trying not to actually *look* at the lake.

But when we get closer, it's clear it's a kid stuck out there, thrashing and splashing, clearly struggling to stay afloat. Everything's happening so fast that no one really knows what to do, but then I see Ian move past me in a blur and there's another splash before I figure out what's going on.

He moves with a purpose, his strong body pushing through the overgrown weeds on the bottom of the lake. This time of year, it's still a little too cold for swimming, so the plants haven't been trampled down by bathers and they're probably what's making it so hard for the poor kid to break the surface. But then Ian's got his arms around him and he's pulling him to shore where an overly-thankful mother scoops her child to her chest, as a brusque woman pushes in, saying she's the doctor.

I snatch a nearby towel off the ground and hand it to Ian, seeing how pale his skin is, that slightly blue tinge already taking over from the chill.

"That was amazing," I say, breathless, more than a little turned on, but also kind of terrified for Ian's sake. I can't believe he just jumped in there like that without any hesitation.

I watch him drag the towel over his body, my mouth watering as my eyes follow the terrycloth. I wish I could towel him off myself, or actually have the courage to offer to do it, but that's not me. That's not something that meek and timid Grant Rainier would ever do.

"Why did you just jump in like that?" I ask, still in disbelief. The idea of going anywhere *near* that lake terrifies me, and Ian just plunged in like he did it every day.

He shrugs, raking the towel through his short dark hair. "I didn't think about it, to be honest."

Of course he didn't. Talk about perfect. Built the way he is, looking the way he does, but also compassionate and brave? How am I supposed to *not* fantasize about that?

I don't get a chance to say anything else to him because suddenly there's a crowd forming around him, fawning over him, congratulating him and passing him beers and clapping him on the back. Ian accepts the praise with humility and grace, but I'm not able to catch his eye again.

Just as well. Knowing me, it was probably only a matter of time before I made a complete fool out of myself anyway. He's Trevor's best friend. I need to remember that. Anything I say to Ian is likely going to get back to Trevor and that just means endless teasing from my older brother.

Besides, I don't think Ian is gay. I don't really remember him dating much when we were growing up, but he is eight years older than me and I *did* have a crush on him, so I wouldn't put it past myself to block out the memories of any girlfriends he'd had.

Still, no matter what I tell myself, for the rest of the day my eyes are roaming around the party aimlessly until they land on Ian.

"What are you doing over here being antisocial?" my

cousin May says, coming up behind me and shoving my shoulder playfully.

"Hey," I say, grinning.

She wraps me in a big hug. "I feel like I haven't seen you in *forever*."

"It's been a couple of years," I say, nodding and chuckling. May's the baby of the other half of the Rainier family. My Uncle Derick's kid. May's a few years younger than me, even, and should be getting ready to head off to college soon -- if her mom doesn't try to stop her like mine did me. .

"How are you liking being back in the old hometown?"

I shrug. "I just got here a couple of days ago."

"Your mom driving you crazy yet?"

"Only a little," I laugh. Out of the Rainier matriarchs, I definitely think my mom is more upset about the idea of her babies all growing up and leaving the nest. Aunt Aislynn couldn't be happier from what I've heard. Not that I've been to visit them either yet.

"You just wait. You're moving to the city, aren't you?"

"In a few months," I say with a nod.

She nods too, sipping on her soda. "Well, don't let her talk you out of it. I've heard her scheming and trying to find a way to keep you here, but if going to the city is what you really want, don't let anyone get in your way."

"Yeah, I know," I say, eyes drifting over to Ian again. If he were the one wanting me to stay in Umberland I don't know that I'd be so resistant.

"So what are you doing over the summer?" she asks, nudging me. "Got any wild plans?"

I snort-laugh and it surprises me so much that I'm actually embarrassed, but then May laughs at *that* and we're both laughing.

"Come on, it hasn't been *that* long, has it? Me? Wild plans?" I laugh. "You're barking up the wrong tree."

And again, my eyes land on Ian. I don't even mean to do it. But he's just like a beacon. A dripping wet beacon, golden tan, his clothes sticking to the contours of every last muscle. Water traveling in streams down his chest, below his waistband...

"So?" May says, frowning at me, turning and squinting. "What are you looking at?"

I snap out of it, shake my head, lick my lips, my whole mouth dry as a desert.

"Nothing," I lie. "I just thought I saw something weird."

May's frown just gets deeper and I can tell she doesn't buy it. I swear, sometimes cousins are as bad as siblings. At least in our family.

"What's going on with you? You're all distracted."

"Am not."

"Are too."

I sigh. "I'm sorry, there's just been a lot going on since I've been back and I'm a little exhausted. It makes me kind of a space cadet."

Her face softens and she looks sympathetic. "You probably didn't even want to come to this dumb thing, but your mom made you, huh?"

"Well, not exac—"

"I'm gonna go get you a beer and then we should ditch this place."

"Ditch it and go where?"

She nibbles on her bottom lip, tucking a golden curl behind her ear. "That's a good question..."

"May," Ryan, the oldest of the Rainier cousins, runs up to her panting, dropping a heavy hand on her shoulder and making her knees buckle. "I need your help."

She pulls a face at him. "You mean one of Umberland's finest needs the help of his baby sister? Whatever for?"

"First, I'm off-duty," he says, narrowing his eyes at her.

"Second, Barb actually likes you. Can you please come run interference?"

May sighs and rolls her eyes.

"Don't ever get married, Grant."

Ryan just makes a face at her. "You don't have to be so dramatic."

"Says the guy needing a buffer to talk to his ex-wife," she tosses back.

"Can you just do me a favor without making a big deal about it?" he pleads.

May gives me an apologetic look and I shake my head.

"Don't worry about it," I say, waving her off. "Go do what you have to do. I'll be in town for a few months."

She sighs, still looking like she feels awful about the whole thing as she gives me a tight squeeze.

"A rain check though, yeah?" she asks.

I nod. "Definitely."

Like I said, cousins may be as bad as siblings, but that means they've got their good traits too. At least I know I'll always have people looking out for me and on my side in Umberland. I know I'll always have a home here.

But it's not where I want to be forever. I majored in Urban Planning and Development for a reason. I like cities. I like the engineering and intricate thought process that goes into making a city operate as smoothly as possible for all citizens. I can't wait to make my stamp on the world, and I know that's not going to happen in Umberland.

But I'm still young. I'm only twenty-three. Delaying my career for one summer isn't going to hurt anything, and after talking to Ian, I'm starting to think the summer at home isn't going to be nearly as bad as I anticipated.

I'm thinking about leaving the barbecue when my eyes scan the crowd one more time, picking out Ian's tall, solid frame easily. But this time when I spot him, I swear I catch him looking at me too, and a little thrill shivers down my spine.

I'm sure it's nothing. I'm sure I'm imagining things. But I'm also *sure* he was just checking me out.

IAN

"Well hey there, superstar," Barb says from behind the bar as I walk in. That's a little joke of hers. One I don't think is so funny, but it seems to amuse the hell out of her. I'm not really sure if it's more in reference to my career as a professional baseball player, or the rescue by the lake—since everyone around town has been bringing that up for the last few days. I really don't think either one's a very big deal and I definitely don't need a nickname.

"What'll it be?" she adds, leaning forward over the bar, showing off the low cut of her top. I guess as the youngest bartender in town she needs to play the part, but someone needs to step up to the plate soon. Barb's not really pulling off the young chick look anymore.

Not that she was ever my type to begin with.

"Jameson and a Bud," I say, sliding into a booth away from her. At least this way she won't be able to pester me while I wait for Trevor to show up.

"You got it," she calls.

It's been a few days since the Memorial Day shindig down

by the lake and I haven't seen Grant since then, but he's supposed to start working with me tomorrow. I don't know why I'm nervous about it. It's been years and years since I've seen little Grant, but he's not so little now. He's grown up. And he's filled out.

And he's definitely caught my eye.

But he's my best friend's brother, so I've got to tread carefully. If I were smart, I'd avoid treading at all. But I've never claimed to be smart. Cocky, yes. Talented, definitely. Amazing in bed? Without a doubt.

But smart? No. Never. I make *very* stupid choices. Especially when it comes to men.

"Here you go, sweetheart. Want me to start you a tab?"

"Yeah, thanks," I say, handing my credit card over to Barb, then downing the shot. It burns, but it's that familiar comforting burn that feels like seeing an old friend again. You can't beat the Irish when it comes to making whiskey.

Beer on the other hand… I sip my Bud, the light carbonation the perfect follow-up to the shot. Beer I prefer to be American-made.

"You haven't been waiting long, have you?" Trevor says, sliding into the other side of the booth. He looks a little flustered like he was in a hurry to get here, but he was the one to ask me to meet him, so I don't know why he'd be in a rush.

Besides, we're just hanging out. It's not like I've got anywhere else to be.

"Nah, don't worry about it," I say. I see him eye the empty shot glass, but he doesn't say anything if he thinks I'm lying about how long I've been here.

"Hey Barb, can I get what he's having?" Trevor calls over to the bar. Barb looks up, and for just a split second her face changes. She looks at Trevor like something on the bottom of her shoe. But it's gone so fast I'm almost not sure I saw it at all. Or I wouldn't have been if Trevor didn't huff just as she did it.

"What's that all about?" I ask, sipping my beer. Barb's getting his drink ready, but she's taking her time with it. "She's not still mad about the time we put food coloring in her tanning lotion, is she?"

"That wasn't Barb, that was Sheila, and for the record *she* is still pissed," he says.

"What's Barb's deal, then?" I'm pretty sure she would have served me three times over in the time it's taking her to pour Trevor a shot.

He shakes his head. "Don't worry about it. Just family drama."

I frown, my eyes sliding back to Barb, who's finally coming over to us with Trevor's drinks.

"Thirteen dollars," she snaps.

Trevor pulls out some cash from his wallet and hands it to her. "Keep it."

She almost looks like she wants to refuse the tip, but she holds her tongue and walks away.

"That's not family drama. That's personal," I prod. She didn't even give him the option of opening a tab.

He rolls his eyes. "Barb isn't really supportive of my *life-style choices*," he sneers, taking a long swig from his beer.

My jaw clenches. There's only one thing that means and it's bullshit. Trevor and I have both made those same *lifestyle choices*—not that it was a choice for either of us—but the only difference is that he's openly out and I'm not. So he's getting mistreated while Barb bends over backward to keep me happy.

I can't help but wonder what her nickname for me might be if she knew. I doubt it would be as flattering as superstar, as stupid as that name already is.

"It really doesn't matter," he says, seeing my hand balled

into a fist. I want to defend my friend. I want to tell Barb exactly what I think about her narrow-minded attitude, but it's a small town, so what do I expect really? Besides, it's a *small* town. It's not exactly crawling with bars and I don't want to burn bridges at the only decent one.

"It's bullshit, and it does matter," I growl, but we both know I'm not going to do anything about it. It's not like me picking a fight would change her mind anyway.

Trevor shrugs and downs his shot. "It is what it is. How are things going at the camp? I haven't been up there in forever," he says wistfully.

"Camp Eagle Peak is not quite what you remember." It's actually not much of anything anymore. Mr. Harris, the previous owner, died six years ago, and it's basically been left to vandals and nature since then. It's not pretty.

"Oh man, we used to practically *live* in that lake. There was that rope swing from the sycamore… shit, I think Parris might have broken his arm jumping off of that thing."

I laugh, shaking my head. "Is there a bone that boy *hasn't* broken?"

Trevor rolls his eyes. "If the stories I hear every Thanks-giving are to be believed, there's *one*," he groans.

That just makes me laugh harder. I'm pretty sure Trevor's giant family exasperates him, but as someone with no siblings and no living parents… The stories never cease to fascinate me. I'm not saying that I necessarily *want* a family as crazy as Trevor's, but there are definitely worse things. Worse options for family, for sure. The Rainiers are always there for each other, no matter what. And when you've got a safety net that big, I'd guess it feels like you can take on the world.

Then again, that might just be me romanticizing things. The grass is always greener, after all.

"You think it's funny. He's annoying as hell," Trevor says.

"I've definitely got my work cut out for me at the camp," I say, thinking about Grant again. Then jumping from one thought to the next, I ask, "What's the dating scene looking like these days?"

He arches his brow at me.

I shrug. "I'm tired of living in the dark. I came back to get away from that. It's time to stop being scared of who I am."

That seems to appease him. He takes another drink of his beer, staring off into the far distance like he's conjuring up the list from the recesses of his mind.

"There's a few guys... Not a ton, mind you. It's a small town. There's Eli... He's not the friendliest... a nurse though, so maybe there's more to him than it seems." He pauses long enough to take another drink. "I don't know if he's out yet, but the bagger kid down at Meloni's is... well, he's too young for you."

"Young's not necessarily bad..." I say, again thinking about Grant.

Damn it. I need to stop that. Trevor's going to see right through me if I'm not careful.

He makes a face at me, but then seems to write it off as just another weird thing I've said.

"I went out with a teacher a couple of times... Perez... Uh... Jonathon. Yeah. Jonathon Perez. Don't ask me what he teaches."

"Wasn't going to. Anyone else?"

"I don't think so... Oh, wait, I forgot that Caleb moved back. His uncle, Old Man Pierce, finally retired and left the shop to him."

My eyebrows go up. "Caleb with the smile, Caleb?"

Trevor nods, laughing. "That's the one."

But he still doesn't mention Grant. I guess I don't know for sure that Grant is gay, but I've always gotten the impression from him. And I don't think I imagined the sizzle and spark between us at the barbecue the other day. There is something there, and it's not just a guy excited to get a job offer.

The only way to know for sure is to ask.

"Is Grant gay?" I blurt out, not even putting any finesse on it.

Trevor narrows his eyes at me and drops his beer bottle to the table with a loud clatter. Barb sends a look our way, but nothing more than that.

"Yeah, he came out pretty recently. But don't even think about it, Ian. He's my little brother. No."

I hold up my hand. "I'm just curious. We're going to be working together for a while. Just the kind of thing I should know, don't you think?"

His eyes are still narrowed at me as he brings the bottle up to his lips again. "Mm-hmm," he grunts.

Barb brings me another beer without me asking.

"Trevor will have one too," I say, "on my tab."

I watch as she grinds her teeth before smiling. "Sure thing, superstar." This time, it's definitely not a friendly nickname.

"You should be careful," Trevor says as she walks away.

"I already told you, I'm not going after your brother," I joke. I'm hoping to make light of his suspicions, but the joke falls flat. He just glowers at me and I'm pretty sure he's even *more* suspicious now. Great. Good job, Ian.

"So what are the plans at the camp?" he asks, making a clear move to change the subject. That's cool. I don't need to stick my foot in my mouth any more than I already have.

"First things first...fixing up my cabin. I'm basically roughing it right now. After that, I'd like to get the dock fixed up so it's not a death trap. There are a few big projects, but mostly it's a mountain of tiny shit that's just too much to do on my own."

Even as I say it, I can't help imagining Grant at the camp with me, working hard, sweating in the afternoon heat, peeling his shirt off, glistening in the sun.

I lick my lips, blood rushing southward so fast it leaves me almost lightheaded. I think about dragging him back into my cabin after a day of hard work and taking him in the shower, slathering him with soap, his fingers clawing at the tile walls, steam coiling around both of us.

"What do you say?" Trevor asks.

I blink. I have no idea what he's talking about. But I do know I'm hard as a fucking rock thinking about his baby brother. *Shit*. I hope he doesn't want to get out of here anytime soon. That would be hard to explain.

"About…?"

He gives me a look and sighs. "I said if you've got that much stuff, I could probably find some downtime to come help."

Just what I need. My best friend cockblocking me.

Actually, maybe I *did* need it. But I'm not known for smart decisions. Not at all.

"I thought you were booked out for months and months. What's this about downtime?"

"Shut up, asshole. Even if you weren't doing this project, I'd want to hang out with you now that you're back in town. So if I've got to do some painting or something while you provide the beers, it's not all that different, is it?"

"Who said anything about me providing beers?"

Trevor laughs, giving me the finger. "You're going to regret not taking me up on it when you realize what a shitty painter Grant is."

"*Now* you tell me," I say.

Trevor just laughs more. "He's your fuckin' problem now, man."

I try to hide my grin by drinking my beer, but it's too big to hide. Grant Rainier my problem?

I think I can live with that.

GRANT

*M*emories flood in as I drive down the dirt and gravel road under the worn and weathered 'Camp Eagle Peak' sign. There were so many summers spent here, it's hard to believe that it was so long ago. It feels like yesterday.

But it's clear that it was a lot longer than that by the state of things. I'm frowning as I pull up out in front of the main cabin. This place has definitely seen better days. *A lot* better.

The cabins look like they've been hosting teenage parties for the last few years. There's trash everywhere, remnants of fires from long ago, and there's graffiti, too. What the teenagers didn't ruin, nature's taken over. Thick spiderwebs hang in the windows and doorways, and climbing weeds are starting to work through the log walls. The big archway that used to grace the camp's entrance is falling down and rotting now, the sign barely hanging on, and a colony of wasps is taking up residence in one of the crumbling sections of wood.

When I was a kid, this place was so much more... *vibrant*. It was alive with people and activity, sunshine and laughter.

Families making memories and enjoying the best nature had to offer.

Now it just feels… sad. Like it's been forgotten.

"There you are!" Ian says, appearing from within the trees. "Right on time." He's smiling, but I can't seem to smile back. I'm still looking around at the state of things, and I can't lie, it's looking rough. It's looking really rough. Like I'm not sure we can save it rough.

"Everything okay?" he asks, frowning. Guess I'm pretty transparent.

"I don't know. This place is…"

"It's a lot, I know," he says. "But that's what we're here for. To fix it up and bring it back to its former glory."

"Are you sure that's even *possible?*" I ask, making a face. "This is a *big* job, Ian."

He grins. "Afraid of handling a big job, Grant?"

Whether he means the innuendo or not, it hits me full force and my face is turning fifty shades of red in an instant.

"Come on, let me show you what I've been working on and what I've got planned," he says, waving for me to follow. He's smiling, but I swear it's a smile that says, "Yeah, I know I just made you think about how big my dick is." It's a smile that spells trouble for me if I'm not careful.

"So, obviously, the cabin is priority. I've got the plumbing mostly done, so I think I should be able to move in soon, but there's still a lot to do. Then over here, I want to have a little stage, with seating spread out over this field. There's some old benches tossed in a clearing I can show you. I think most of them are salvageable."

I nod, determined to focus on what he's saying even though I keep getting distracted by the way his lips move, the way the tight white T-shirt he's wearing clings to every muscle, not even attempting to hide how perfect he is underneath it.

And don't even get me started on those jeans. They look like they were custom-made for him and they're doing a hell of a job showing off his ass and his package. I'm surprised I've heard as many of his words as I have, to be honest.

"There's a copse of pines out this way that I think would be the perfect place for a ropes course. Of course that's getting further into the future."

I keep following him around the camp, the sound of his voice washing over me, the warm late-spring air lulling me into a feeling of peace and contentment. The sun is bright, still making its ascent, and the sky is a crisp blue, cloudless and perfect. I couldn't really ask for a better day to be outside with Ian.

But this isn't just some casual hang out. I'm supposed to be working for him, and I need to focus. I need to pay attention to what's going on and what he's saying. I don't want him to think I'm some kind of airhead.

"This is another priority," he says. I realize we're nearly at the water's edge and I take a step back as he strolls out on the rickety old dock.

"It's more solid than it seems, but it's still got some spots over here that we'll need to rip out completely and rebuild," he says, crouching down to examine it.

I take another step back, casting my eyes around for an excuse before I land on the lifeguard tower. Perfect.

While Ian's looking at the dock and pointing out issues, I'm looking at the lifeguard tower, trying not to have a complete and total meltdown.

Water, rushing in. All around me. Up, down, none of it made any sense. My lungs burning as I kicked and opened my mouth to scream only to swallow a ton of water. My heart racing, my vision fading, the last bit of light going out...

"What'd you find over here?" Ian asks, his hand on my

shoulder. I jump at his sudden appearance, trying to shake myself out of the old memory.

I *almost* drowned in that lake. Almost is the key word. It didn't get me and I'm not going to let it.

"Uh…" My heart's still racing from the memory and I take a few quick breaths to try and calm myself down. The last thing I need is for Ian to see me have some kind of panic attack and then treat me as a fragile, breakable thing forever. I look over the tower, scrambling for something.

"These screws over here look too close to the edge of the board. And this one's load-bearing, so that's just asking for a catastrophic failure when someone jumps off of it the wrong way," I say quickly, thankful I found something to cover my ass.

"Good catch," he says, squeezing my shoulder before letting go. I know it's crazy, but I swear that spot is tingling from where he touched me, heat spreading into my bloodstream, making me hot and itchy under my own skin.

We wander around the camp a bit more, finding additional projects, Ian going on and on about his plans to make this place the camp of his teenage dreams. It's freaking adorable and I know I'm probably staring at him, but *come on.* I can't resist a guy that's passionate about something. It's just so endearing.

As we finish the circuit around the camp, Ian pulls out his keys. I'm disappointed that he's calling it a day so soon, but he's the boss.

"Wanna come to the lumberyard with me? I'm gonna need a lot of wood."

"Yeah you are," I say, but it's not the words that makes it awful, it's the tone I inadvertently use. The tone that says I'm clearly suggesting where he can get some wood.

Jesus, what is wrong with me? It's like the minute I'm near Ian, I forget how to think about anything other than sex.

23

Maybe all those years of masturbating and fantasizing about him really did mess me up.

But he just gives me one of those smiles. The smiles that make my breath catch, my heart melt. The smiles I almost can't stand to look at because he's just *too* attractive. He gives me one of those smiles and unlocks his truck, jerking his head toward it.

"Come on, let's go."

I feel like he can see right through me, but I don't hate the feeling. Probably because he keeps looking at me like he likes what he sees. There's just something… appreciative when he looks over at me, something that softens in his eyes, and it's driving me crazy because I don't know if it's really there or if I'm just imagining things I want to see.

"So Urban Planning, huh?" he asks, starting up the truck, heading off down the bumpy road.

"Yep."

"I don't really know what that means, you know," he says, tossing me another effortless smile. I grip the handhold in the door and grit my teeth. Luckily, the rutted road is a good enough cover for me.

"It's uh… Well, basically, I'd look at a city and… plan it."

His smile just grows. "That makes sense. It's right there in the title, huh?"

I know he's making fun of me, but it doesn't feel malicious. It's light and teasing and it's *working*. I feel myself relaxing.

"Who do you think decides where the parks go? Or the schools? Or where the commercial and residential areas should be? The person that brings up old neighborhoods, makes sure public transportation reaches the places it's needed, ensures the supply of water, electricity, and sewage services? All that stuff and way more ends up on the desk of the Urban Planner."

His eyebrows go up and he looks actually… impressed?

"Big dreams, kid," he says.

"Coming from you," I tease back.

He grunts at that. "What made you want to get into Urban Planning, then?"

I shrug. "It seemed fun. I spent a lot of time as a kid playing *SimCity*."

"Nerd," he says, grinning at me.

"Guilty as charged." I shrug again. "What made you come back to Umberland?"

His hands tighten on the wheel for just a second. I'm not sure I was supposed to see that, so I pretend I didn't.

"Just thought it was time to come home, you know?"

I make a face. "Not me. I kind of had to be guilted into spending the summer back here."

He laughs, but it almost sounds bitter. "You're young. You'll understand."

"Ugh," I scoff, rolling my eyes. "Don't give me that bullshit."

He gives me a curious look.

"That 'I'm the baby of the family so everyone has to remind me how young I am all the time' bullshit. I'm an adult; I have a degree and I've lived on my own for years now…"

"I'm sorry," he says, and it sounds surprisingly sincere. "You're definitely an adult. It's kind of hard to remember that. You know the last time I saw you, you were what…twelve?"

I sigh. "Fourteen. That growth spurt took forever to show up." But even at fourteen, I was plenty old enough to see twenty-two-year-old Ian and know that it was exactly what I wanted.

Some things never change apparently.

"Your brother was the same way," he laughs. "I was a foot taller than him until halfway through sophomore year."

"I don't remember that," I say, frowning. Trevor always seemed like a giant to me.

"You were just a kid then."

"Eight years made way more of a difference back then than it does now," I say, catching myself being suggestive again before I can even stop it.

But I see something in Ian's eyes. I see him flick them down even if it's so fast he probably didn't think I would.

"You're right," he says, almost growling.

I swear the tension between us is sizzling hot, but we're both just trying to pretend it doesn't exist. I don't know how long I can go on like this.

Once we're down in the valley at the hardware store, I step out of the truck and suddenly the fresh air clears my head. I don't feel backed into a corner by Ian's piercing smiles and intoxicating outdoorsy scent. I feel like I can finally breathe and think again.

We each grab one of the huge flat trolleys and head off into the lumberyard. Ian's got a shopping list as long as my arm and we slowly work our way through it, moving as a team to load the trolleys up and double-check the counts.

By the time we get to the checkout, all the weird intimidation I had been feeling around him is gone. This little shopping trip was just so domestic and natural that it's impossible to deny. Ian's not just my older brother's hot friend that I've had a crush on forever. He's a nice guy. He's easy to talk to. We kind of have this unspoken thing between us that lets us do things together without either one of us having to say what we're doing. Like lifting a huge beam of wood or something. We just work together.

And in working together like that, I've come to realize today that Ian's not really that older than me. He might be more experienced than me—okay, he's *definitely* that—but we're equals in a lot of other ways.

Surprisingly—or maybe not at all—realizing that Ian and I are equals just makes me want him *more*. It's not some forbidden illicit thing. It's real and possible and that thought has me salivating. Eager.

"Did you find everything you needed today?" The familiar voice surprises me and I look up from where I'm gathering lumber."Hey Uncle Derick," I say, surprised that he's manning the register himself. He's usually got one of his kids working in here so he can be on the farm. Though, from what I've heard, he's got more help up there these days. I'm sure mom appreciates him keeping Sawyer close for her.

Ian chuckles at the question. "I sure hope so. There's an awful lot here to be missing anything more."

"What're you working on?" he asks, looking at me. If I didn't know better, I'd think he sees right through me and my attraction to Ian. But he's too much like my dad for that. It's just polite conversation, I'm sure.

"He's fixing up the camp at Eagle Peak," I say. "I needed something to keep busy with over summer, so I'm helping him out."

Uncle Derick's eyebrows go up, and he looks so much like my dad that it's almost weird. I hope I never look that much like Trevor after all the times I've called him ugly. I'd never hear the end of it.

"Well, it's about time someone did something with it. Good for you," he says, scanning through all of Ian's purchases with lightning speed. "All right... And with the family discount, that comes to six eighty-three, seventy-four."

"Family discount?" Ian asks, frowning.

"You're with Grant here," he says.

"We're working together," I emphasize.

Uncle Derick nods, waving my comment off. "That's what I said. David? Can you come help these boys load up their purchases?

A guy pops his head out of the back room and smiles.

"Sure thing boss," he says, hurrying out, wiping his hands on the wrinkled apron he's wearing.I see something in the way he looks at Ian that makes me clench my fists. The way he's looking at him makes a little voice pop up in the back of my head screaming *mine!*

But that's *ridiculous*. Ian is not mine.

"Well, if you find you missed anything, you could always come back. I'd be happy to help you out," Derick says.

"I'm sure I'll be making plenty of trips down here this summer. Me or Grant, that is," he says, waving my direction.

"Was good seeing you, tell your folks I said hello for me, won't you Grant?"

I nod. "Sure thing."

"And don't be a stranger."

I wave as we head out with David -- though I don't think we actually need the help, he's coming anyway, and Ian hasn't told him not to.

"Wow, that's a nice truck," the guy says, focusing on Ian. The way he's looking at him, he's *obviously* interested. I'm not jealous. I'm just...*annoyed*. I feel territorial and I don't want anyone else making eyes at him."You're that guy that just moved back to town, aren't you?" David asks, as we're all loading wood into the back of the truck.

Ian shrugs. "One of them. There's a few of us."

He grins. "But you're the baseball player, right? Who'd you play for again?"

Ian tosses in the last of the wood and slams the tailgate. "Have a good day," he grumbles, clearly dismissing the kid.

Maybe he finally caught on that the guy was flirting. Took him long enough. But I don't really know anyone that ends up in this bad of a mood because of some unsolicited flirting. Especially that minor.

"Let's go," he says, leaving me to pass the trolleys off to a bewildered-looking David.

I shove them away and scramble to catch up with him and get in the truck.

Something just got under Ian's skin.

Was it David?

Was it me, cramping his style?

Or was it baseball?

I don't really know a lot about the circumstances under which he left the game. As far as I know, it was a voluntary retirement, though it did seem to surprise a lot of people.

I never really thought to ask Trevor about why Ian was retiring at thirty-one, but suddenly I'm very curious. It seems young, even for a career in professional sports. And from what I know of him, he's had a fairly successful career. I don't really follow sports, but I think I'd at least know if he were a dismal failure.

Or maybe I wouldn't. Maybe that's the big secret.

Somehow, I don't think so.

I want to ask him if everything's all right, but I don't know if we're at that point yet. I don't know if I can ask him something that personal and not have him shut down or get angry.

But I also don't know that I can see him being this closed off and not say something.

I wait until we're back on the main road to break the silence.

"Sorry if my uncle was weird..."

He looks over, his eyebrows going up. "No," he says simply.

I frown, not knowing what's up his butt.

"The kid seemed interested in you," I say, holding my breath for a moment.

He grumbles something. "It happens. People are nosy."

"You think that was it?" I ask.

He shrugs. "What else would it be?"

"I thought that was pretty obvious."

He arches a brow at me but doesn't pull his eyes away from the road. "What's that?"

I sigh, shaking my head. "Are you that oblivious? He was obviously flirting with you."

Ian seems genuinely surprised by that suggestion. "Why would he do that?" he asks incredulously.

I've got a laundry list of reasons that pops into my head immediately. Ian's attractive, he's compassionate, he's successful, he's got a smile that makes my stomach do somersaults and a twinkle in his eye that makes my mouth dry.

Not to mention what he does *south* of my waistband.

I don't know how he can't see that he's the total package. Maybe he's just screwing with me. Trying to get me to lavish him with compliments.

Well that's not going to happen. No sirree. I'm not going to let him corner me into admitting how much I want him. I might be young, but I can still spot a trap when it's covered in neon signs.

"Well, you're kind of a famous athlete, aren't you? That's probably enough of a reason for some."

"That's a stupid reason," he mutters.

I stretch my legs out, leaning back in the seat, trying to approach the subject carefully. I don't want him to pull back on me. I'm genuinely curious now.

"So Trevor never told me... Why'd you retire?" I'm trying to sound casual. Light. Like it's no big deal.

Ian's not having it. His face goes hard, his hands tightening on the wheel.

"I wanted to retire. Do I need more of a reason?"

I swallow, his gaze boring into me, making me feel like a kid who's in trouble. I shake my head. "No, I guess you don't."

"You're right. I don't."

So much for that conversation. Guess I've found a sore spot. I'll have to tread lightly from here on out.

IAN

*W*e ride back to the camp in silence and I'm cursing myself internally the whole way for snapping at Grant the way I did. I'm just on edge. Not just with the subject of why I left the league, but with him too. *He* puts me on edge because there's something about him that makes me feel uncertain about myself and what I'm doing.

Where I'm normally confident, or, as some would say, cocky, Grant has me second-guessing myself. I can't stop sending sideways glances at him while I drive, but he's quiet as a church mouse.

At the camp, we start to unload things, and I'm struck again by how well we seem to work together. I never spent a ton of time with Trevor's baby brother when we were growing up, but there's no denying what a capable man he's grown into. Strong too.

He's strong, but he's not built like me. Grant's all lean muscle like a runner. He's tall, but narrower, and he's still young enough that it shows in his face. He's full of youth and vigor and his unruly sun-kissed hair only adds to the image.

"Where do you want all this?" he asks, nudging a pile of

plywood. It's the first he's spoken to me since I shut him down in the truck.

"Over by where the stage will be," I say, gesturing.

He nods and sets off without saying anything else.

I want to say something, maybe even apologize for earlier, but right now there's just too much work to do. I can't take the time to think about it.

We get everything unloaded and Grant speaks to me a couple more times, but only to ask where something goes or what I want him to do next. It's strictly work and it has me grinding my teeth.

I want more from him. I know I have no right to ask for it. But I do. I want so much more. And it's wrong. I know it's wrong. He's my best friend's little brother and Trevor's already told me to keep my distance.

But that just makes me want him more. Forbidden fruit is so much sweeter.

It's not just that I can't have him that makes me want him, obviously, but it sure as hell doesn't help me forget him.

"Now what?" he asks once we've got everything unloaded. He's sweating and the way the sun glints off his slightly tanned skin has me licking my lips, following the trail of sweat as it drips under his collar.

"Guess we'll start working on the cabin," I say quickly, snapping out of my thoughts. Fantasizing about him isn't going to make this job go any faster.

He follows me in to the main house where I'll eventually be living. Right now, I've got a tent set up right outside. At least I've finally worked out all the problems with the plumbing so we have a bathroom and I can take hot showers like a civilized human.

"So, obviously, we need to clear out all the trash and debris and stuff. And then I'd like us to just start ripping out rotted boards and shit to see what we're really working with."

Grant nods, already moving to the dust-caked windows to open them.

The window's jammed, and he's putting a lot of effort into trying to open it, making these grunting noises that are going *straight* to my cock.

"Here, let me," I say, offering to help on the other side.

"It's just…" he grunts again and the window budges without my help. "Frame's swollen shut."

"Yeah, there's a lot of stuff like that around here. Hope you're not afraid of spiders."

He follows my gaze and spots the big jumping spider in the corner.

"You stay out of my way and I'll stay out of yours," he says to it. He's having a more meaningful conversation with a spider than with me. I should never have snapped at him the way I did. It's clearly still bugging him and this is not the start to a summer-long job working with him that I hoped for.

Still, I can tell that he's trying to give me a wide berth, so I do the same. Maybe he's looking at me like I'm a jumping spider and he just wants to stay out of my way.

We set to work, clearing the last of the old crap out of the cabin, tossing it all in a big pile far enough away from the buildings that we can light it all on fire later. The steady stream of work makes the day seem like it's going by fast, but when I look at the time a while later, it's only been a couple of hours and already I'm feeling exhausted.

But it's not just the work that's wearing me down. It's the loneliness.

Working alone is one thing. There's this Zen attitude that comes with doing this kind of stuff entirely by yourself. But when you add another person to the mix, there's an expectation that you'll have some company, that the social aspect of having another person would make the work feel lighter. And it was going that way.

But now Grant's shutting me out and it's grating on me. Every time we pass each other without looking, every time we're alone in the cabin for long stretches and there are no words—just grunts of exertion and muttered curses—it makes it worse.

Because being with another person and still feeling alone is way lonelier than just actually being alone.

We get everything cleared out and piled away from the cabin early in the afternoon and it seems as good a time as any to have lunch, but I'm not sure how he's going to respond to the suggestion. Guess there's only one way to find out.

"Wanna grab a bite? We could head down to the diner and—"

"I brought lunch with me, but if you wanna take a break, go ahead," he says. "I can keep working on stuff till you get back."

For a split second, I bristle at his response, the implication that I can't handle the hard work a slap in the face. But I think about it for a second longer and I don't think that's what Grant meant.

"Come on, let's take a break. We'll eat here then. I've got stuff."

Grant stops tugging on the board he's working on, wiping the back of his arm across his forehead with a sigh. He drops the claw hammer, seeming to accept defeat, and heads out of the cabin.

I don't know why his reaction just annoys me. I'm trying to break the ice. Trying to develop some kind of cama-raderie so we're not working together for ten weeks in silence.

That's probably what he was trying to do with baseball, a sneering little voice in the back of my head says.

I clench my jaw, knowing the voice is right. I've got to make this up to Grant somehow or we're never getting past this.

Grant goes to his car and pulls out a little insulated lunch box. He looks all around for somewhere to sit and there's nowhere near the cabin. I don't have a table or chair, or even a stump for him.

But I do have a truck. So I put the tailgate down.

"It's not the most comfortable, but it's somewhere to sit," I say.

He shrugs, sits, and pulls out a sandwich.

Before I join him, I head over to my little dry storage area, locked up tight against bears. I grab some jerky, nuts, dried fruit, that kind of thing. I've got little individual pots of peanut butter and some pretzels. Seems good enough for a lunch to me. I'll just make sure I have a hot meal for dinner.

Grant looks at my "lunch" as I hop onto the tailgate next to him, but he doesn't say anything. He just continues eating his sandwich.

Finally, I've had enough. I just can't take it anymore.

"I know I said I didn't want to talk about baseball, but I'll talk about anything else," I say, probably sounding just as desperate as I feel. I don't know what's wrong with me. Why I feel the need for him to acknowledge me so acutely, but *damn* this boy's got me all kinds of twisted up.

Maybe it's just that he's not throwing himself at me. So many people do. Between the fame and fortune, it's hard to know who your real friends are.

But there's no doubt when it comes to the Rainiers. They've basically been my family my whole life.

Which should probably make the decidedly *non-familial* thoughts I'm having about Grant weird. But it doesn't.

I know that Trevor would kill me if he could even get a glimpse of the things I'm imagining doing to his little brother, but damn if that doesn't just make me want it *more*.

Grant sighs.

"I'm sorry if I overstepped…"

"You didn't," I say quickly. "It's just… not something I want to talk about yet."

He nods, takes a bite out of his sandwich.

"So why this camp? There are a lot of other things you could be doing with your retirement."

I nod. "Truth. But I've got nothing but good memories of it. Seems like this place should keep being here for other people to make those kinds of memories."

It's a good answer. A very Miss America answer. It's also mostly bullshit.

Sure, if restoring the camp helps some people make new memories, that's great. But that's not why I'm working on it. It *is* because I've got great memories here, but it's also because all the time I spent here was just so much simpler. Without the outside world, without technology, the city, the tabloids…

Being by myself in the woods was too attractive to resist.

Though now Grant is here, I'm not by myself, and that might be even better.

"That's sweet," he says.

"Don't sound so surprised."

He smirks and gives me a look. "If I recall, you weren't exactly known for being sweet the last time you were in town." He arches a brow and I'm not even sure I know what he's talking about. I guess the confusion's plain on my face because he shakes his head.

"You probably don't even remember, do you?"

"Remember what?" I ask, an unsettling feeling in the pit of my stomach. Trevor and I weren't the nicest of guys back in our day. We liked to think of ourselves as master pranksters, and I didn't remember anything specifically targeting Grant, but I wouldn't put it past us.

"Never mind," he says quickly, shaking his head, shoving his sandwich in his mouth.

I grin. "Oh no. Now you *have* to tell me."

His face turns a bright shade of pink. "It was embarrassing enough the first time!" he says, still working on that bite of sandwich. He swallows. "Don't make me relive the nightmare."

"It couldn't have been *that* bad."

He just looks at me and the serious look on his face makes me snort.

"Okay, come on, you have to tell me."

Grant sighs. "I think I was about twelve? I was old enough to be on to Trevor's crap, so I kept a close watch on all my stuff around him, but you were spending the night and asked if you could use my shampoo since Trevor was supposedly out. When I got it back, it was mixed with dye. Which of course I didn't realize until *after* my skin was purple."

I laugh harder, and Grant cracks a smile, but he's clearly not as amused as I am about the whole thing.

"It's not funny! Mom scrubbed and scrubbed me until all my skin hurt and then I *still* had to go to school all week and get called Barney the Dinosaur for the next... *forever*."

"I'm sorry," I say, but I'm still laughing trying to picture it. I don't remember what he's talking about, but it sounds like exactly the kind of thing we'd do. The kind of prank that we'd think was harmless even though it was kind of mean.

Grant chuckles. "It wouldn't have been so bad coming from Trevor. From him, I was used to that kind of stuff. But from you..."

He cuts himself short and looks away, focusing on the sandwich again.

"You're right. We weren't very nice. It couldn't have been easy growing up with an older brother who was always giving you shit."

He shrugs. "It wasn't all bad." His eyes are lingering on me and I'm not sure why, but I know it's making me want to reach out to him. My fingers are twitchy, wanting to touch him, but I hold back, gnawing on a strip of jerky instead.

Lunch doesn't last much longer, but while it does, Grant shares more stories of Trevor's pranks and the horrors he endured. By the end of it, I'm feeling protective of him—and more than a little annoyed by Trevor's persistence. He has two other siblings to torment, after all.

"I guess we should get back to work," I say with a sigh, looking back toward the cabin, not really wanting to leave the tailgate of the truck now that we're talking and hanging out so naturally.

"Yeah, I doubt you want to be living in a tent forever," he says.

"Not particularly. It would be nice to have an actual roof over my head. And you know… a *bed* maybe?"

His eyes go wide and I can't believe I've gotten that suggestive *again* without meaning to. Don't get me wrong; I consider myself a master at innuendo, but I swear I'm not doing it on purpose this time. It's just coming out and I can't seem to help myself.

"Yeah, a bed is important for things," he says, a flush creeping up his neck as he hops off the tailgate. I can't tell if he's into my inadvertent innuendo or not. He's definitely flustered by it, and it's cute as hell. So maybe I need to keep prodding at that little weak spot. Maybe I'll get somewhere that way.

We get back to working on our separate areas, but thankfully, the conversation doesn't stop.

"So you're just here for the summer?" I ask, verifying

what I've already heard. I don't know how much of a concrete decision it is though. I know what it's like when you first leave college and you're not really sure what you want to do, but you have these big plans. Maybe you do them, but for most people, I think if they go back to their hometown they just end up staying there for one reason or another.

"Yeah," he says. "Honestly, I wouldn't have come back home at all if it weren't for my mom. She's been on my case nonstop about coming back to visit, spending some time at home so she can be with her *baby*. I don't really know what she thinks is going to happen. She's at the diner all the time and we hardly see each other. I don't know where all this quality time is going to magically appear from, but it's making her happy to have me at the breakfast table every morning, I guess."

I smile at the thought. Sheryl Rainier is a force of nature and I couldn't imagine trying to go against her wishes. If she told me she wanted me back in Umberland for a few months, I probably wouldn't have argued either. And I'm not even one of her kids.

"Regardless, thank her for me. I wasn't looking forward to doing all this alone."

Grant shrugs. "I'm happy to have an excuse not to be put to work at the diner again."

I know he's probably just saying that to play it off, to be casual about the situation, but it leaves me feeling... unsettled. Is that all this job is to him? An excuse to not be somewhere else?

I don't know why I think it should be more. It's his first damn day on the job and already I'm acting like there should be some loyalty there.

But is it loyalty to the job I want from Grant, or to me?

"So, long-term plans?" I ask. He's already told me about what he wants to do with his degree, but we haven't really talked about how he plans to make it happen. And Grant's young; maybe he hasn't thought it through that far. Maybe I can help him.

That thought alone leaves a sour taste in my mouth, but I ignore it, shoving it aside.

"Hopefully before the summer's over I'll have a few interviews lined up. The goal is to be starting a new position in August or September, so depending on when and where I get an offer, the tricky part is probably going to be figuring out where I want to live."

"Well, at least if your neighborhood doesn't have the parks and schools you want, you know someone that can make things happen," I tease. But even as he's smiling at my little joke, there's an uneasy feeling in the pit of my stomach.

I don't like thinking about Grant leaving. I don't like thinking about him going back to the city and leaving me out here without ever seeing him again.

I know that's crazy to say, but for the past week I've done nothing but think about him, and thinking about him going away...

My hammer comes down wrong and I don't even realize it until I hear it. The dull *thud* instead of the light metallic *ping*. Grant hears it too and turns before the pain even registers.

But then it hits me like hurricane-force winds.

"*FUCK*," I hiss, my thumb already swelling up, the pressure building under the nail.

"What'd you do?" Grant asks, dropping what he's working on to come and check on me. He takes my hand in his and turns my thumb over and even through the pain I'm still thinking the same thing.

I don't want him to leave Umberland now that I'm here to stay. I'm attracted to him, yes. But I think there might be something even more than that. And I feel guilty about it. He's my best friend's brother. Of *course* I feel guilty about it.

But I also can't deny it. I've spent enough of my life denying who I am and what I feel to do it anymore.

"This is bad, Ian. We should get you down to Dr. Barnes. It might be broken."

"I've had worse," I grunt. "Ever have a ninety-mile-an-hour fast ball slam right into your knuckles?"

He gives me an exasperated look and nudges me toward the door. "Yes, yes. You're a very tough and strong caveman. Who needs a doctor."

I let him lead me out of the cabin, not because I think I need a doctor, but because his concern for me is cute. My thumb is throbbing and screaming in pain, already turning a dozen shades of purple and black, but it doesn't bother me as much because Grant's here and he's taking care of me. Not sure I could ask for a better outcome than that.

GRANT

"This is so silly. I've done so much worse shit to myself and never bothered going to the doctor," Ian grumbles next to me in the waiting room at urgent care. He's like a big angry bear with a thorn in his paw and it's exasperating, but it's also really cute.

"Shush. I wasn't there to make sure you got proper care, so I can't speak to those other times, but I'm here this time and you're going to see a doctor."

He glowers and grumbles some more, but he doesn't actually argue with me or try to make a break for it.

I guess some people might have just brought him to the doctor and left, but that thought didn't even occur to me. I was there when he injured himself and I'm going to be here until he's repaired.

"I don't even understand why there's a wait. We're the only ones here."

"Shh," I whisper-laugh. "They're going to hear you. Do you really want to piss off the person who's going to be poking at your swollen thumb?"

43

He looks down at his hand and grimaces. "I don't have a thumb anymore. I have a plum."

"All the more reason you need to be patient here and let the doctor see you. You don't want to become some *Willy Wonka* cautionary tale, do you?"

"Good point," he says, trying to bend his thumb and wincing. I can tell he doesn't mean to let it show, but it's got to hurt like a bitch.

"Mr. Barrett?" A guy in scrubs pokes his head through the door, looking at the two of us. His eyes narrow, and then Ian stands up.

"That's me."

"Right this way," the nurse says. Ian follows. I do too. I don't even think about it until I'm halfway down the hallway and I realize he never asked me to.

The nurse leads him into an exam room and takes his vitals and the whole time I'm just hovering outside of the doorway like a weirdo because I don't know what I'm doing here. I don't know why I had to follow him back here, but going all the way into the exam room without him asking me to seems like crossing a boundary that even I can't cross.

And just as I'm feeling supremely awkward about loitering in the hallway, I hear Ian call out to me.

"Grant? Are you coming in or not?"

I swallow quickly and try to seem like I'm in control of myself as I step in and close the door behind me. I don't know what it is about him. I keep getting mixed signals. He's hot and then he's cold and then right back to hot again before I know what's hit me. It's giving me whiplash and I don't know what to expect, but I'm also *craving* more of it. More of him.

I know this is bad for me, but God save me, I can't get enough of it.

He's got a blood pressure cuff wrapped tight around his bicep and the nurse pumps it full of air as I take a seat.

"I'm sorry for butting in. I wasn't thinking."

Ian grins at me. "I appreciate the company. I don't like doctors anyway. No offense… Eli," he says to the nurse, reading his name tag.

"None taken. I'm not a doctor." He yanks the stethoscope out of his ears and rips the cuff off of Ian, Velcro loud enough to make me wince. "I'm going to need the bigger cuff for you," he says, walking out of the room without another word.

"I don't think Eli likes me very much," he says, smiling at me.

It's hard to even fake a serious look when he's looking over my way like that. "It's probably because he heard you complaining about waiting."

"Pfft," he scoffs, waving a dismissive hand. "I think Eli doesn't like anyone."

"You don't even know him."

He winks at me, and I have no idea what *that's* supposed to mean. I'm so confused by it that I'm trying to figure out what he meant by it the whole time Nurse Eli comes back and takes his blood pressure and asks him a few questions about his medical history.

"Does it really matter that my grandpa had diabetes when I'm in here for a busted thumb?" he grouses, huffing impatiently.

"Believe it or not, I'm don't ask these questions because I think it's fun," Eli snaps back. "The doctor will see you soon."

He leaves again and Ian seems agitated, but that whole exchange only happened because he's being a baby. At first I thought he was just saying he didn't mind the company to make me feel better, but after watching how he interacted with the nurse, I'm not so sure. He might actually have a problem with doctors. Tough, strong, manly Ian Barrett, afraid of anyone in scrubs.

It's almost funny.

It'll probably be a lot funnier when I'm done dealing with his bout of petulance.

Not that I even consider leaving his side.

"You might want to channel some of that famous charm with the doctor if you wanna leave this place with ten fingers," I suggest.

He tosses a grin over his shoulder at me and I marvel at how he can snap like that, from surly and moody to roguish and charming.

"You think I have charm?"

"Aren't you kind of known for it?"

He rolls his eyes. "Not anymore. The media are fickle."

There it is again. The hint that there's more to the story of why he left baseball than he's letting on. Or maybe I'm just reading too much into it. He doesn't want to share that part of his story with me yet and I shouldn't push. I know I shouldn't. But I want to.

I want to know everything about Ian. All those years crushing on him I never expected to actually hold a conversation with him or spend any amount of time in his company. And now that I'm able to do both, I can't help it. I want to take advantage of it every moment I can.

"Well, I'm sure it's still in you somewhere. Somewhere deep *deep* inside," I say, teasing him. It works. The dark storm cloud that was threatening to roll in moves away and Ian's back.

"I don't know, it's gotta be *really* deep. I doubt anyone's willing to go that far to find it," he says.

I swear it doesn't matter what he says, my mind finds a way to make it sexual. Just the word *deep* coming from Ian's lips like that makes me shiver a little. His deep voice is so smooth and rich that I can't help but be mesmerized by it. He just lulls me into this stupor and I'd probably do whatever he wanted of me. Even here.

There's a knock on the door that snaps me out of it and Dr. Barnes walks in. She smiles at us both and looks over Ian's chart.

"Hi there, I'm Dr. Barnes," she says. I've never met her before, but I know she took over Dr. Alderman's practice a handful of years back and she's the only doctor in town, so it's not like I could have mistaken her for someone else. She shakes Ian's non-injured hand.

"Ian Barrett," he says. "But you already knew that."

"I did," she says, smiling wider.

At least he's not being such a sourpuss right off the bat.

"So I've heard you had a bit of a construction accident?" she asks, lifting her eyebrows. Ian nods and holds up his hand.

"A bit. I don't think it's all that bad, but—"

"Southpaw huh? Yikes," she says, sucking in a breath as she turns his hand over gingerly, running her fingers along his palm. She's practically *caressing* him, making sympathetic noises as she applies gentle pressure to his wounded finger.

"That can't feel good," she says. "What about this?" She tries bending it and he yelps, involuntarily scooting backward on the examination bench.

"Not good then," she says, chuckling. Ian also gives a nervous chuckle, but I see the sheen of sweat on his forehead and I don't know if it's from the pain or from having to be at the doctor's or if it's both, but I desperately want to go over and comfort him.

"We're definitely going to have to get it x-rayed, but it seems broken to me," she says, going to the computer to type something in.

"You've gotta be kidding me," he groans, rubbing his face with his good hand.

"Told you," I say, feeling smugly satisfied. I know I shouldn't be happy that Ian's thumb is broken, but he didn't even want to come to the doctor, so I'm really glad I made him.

"Yeah, yeah, yeah."

"Come on, let's get you down to the lab," Dr. Barnes says, taking him by the elbow, leading him to the door. It definitely feels like she's trying to insert some distance between us and it makes me glare at her, but I'm probably just imagining things. Besides, I don't have any claim to Ian and I need to remember that. As much as I want him to be, he's not mine. And if I want to have any chance of that actually happening, I need to not be such a freak or act jealous.

I follow anyway, determined not to let her have time alone with him if I can help it. She greets the lab tech, hands over Ian's chart, and closes the door behind him. With her on the other side. *My* side.

And it's then that I realize it's not Ian I should worry about being alone with Dr. Barnes, but me.

"You're Trevor Rainier's little brother, aren't you?" she asks, leaning on the wall opposite me, her face friendly enough even though I'm still suspicious.

I nod.

"I went to school with Ian and your brother. A couple of hell-raisers back in their day," she says, smiling fondly. "So Ian's back in town, huh?"

"Yep."

"Any idea for how long?"

I shrug. "Sounds like he's back for good."

Her eyebrows go up and her hips shift subtly. She's interested in Ian. There's no mistaking it. She licks her lips.

"Oh yeah? What's he up to these days?"

Even her voice has changed and it sounds more feminine, like she's trying to find an in and she thinks I'm it.

Well, I hate to break it to her, but I'm pretty sure Ian's gay. Not completely sure. Maybe I'm actually not sure at all and I'm just kind of hopeful, but I know if I say something like that to her I'm just going to look petty and jealous. Like I'm trying to warn her off my boyfriend or something.

And… Well, I kind of *am*. I realize that. I know I have no place to be making judgments about who Ian may or may not date, but I still fold my arms before I answer.

"He bought the old camp out by the lake that Mr. Harris used to own before he passed. We're fixing it up together." I make sure to emphasize the "we," trying to make my point as clear as I possibly can. I'm not going to outright discourage her, but I can do some subtle posturing.

"That explains the smooshed thumb," she says, still smiling though it doesn't go all the way to her eyes anymore.

The door beside her opens and Ian comes back out. Dr. Barnes gives us both a professional smile.

"You can go ahead and go back to the exam room. I'll be in once I've had a look at these."

Once we're out of earshot of the doctor, I lean in to tease Ian. "You've got an admirer."

His brow furrows and I tilt my head slightly. He follows and then looks back at me skeptically.

"The doctor?"

I nod. "Apparently you went to high school together?"

He snorts, quiet chuckles rumbling through his muscled chest. "That's flattering, but she's not really my type."

"Oh?" I ask, my heartbeat picking up. It's the perfect opportunity and I know I have to take it, but already my mouth's dry and my palms are sweaty. "What is your type?"

We're back in the exam room and Ian sits on the table, me back in the chair. He shrugs casually.

49

"Athletic, but not a gym rat, blond, great smile, caring, ambitious. You know, just... different than her."

The doctor's a brunette, but other than that, I don't know how he could decipher any of the other stuff from his brief interaction with her.

But there's someone else he could easily be describing: *me*.

I know it's crazy to think he's talking about me, but I can't help the warm glow that fills me, the satisfaction I feel all the way to my toes. It's so easy to lose myself in the fantasy of this guy I've had a thing for *forever* finally looking at me and seeing something worthwhile.

But I can't lose myself in that fantasy, because it's just that. It's a fantasy. It's not reality. At least not in any tangible sense. If Ian's talking about me—and that's a *big* if—he still hasn't made any kind of move. I can't expect it to mean anything.

Hell, for all I know, he might be completely, one hundred percent straight.

I don't even say anything before Dr. Barnes is back.

"That was quick," Ian says.

She sticks the plastic sheet with the x-ray up on an old-school light board on the wall and flips the lights.

"Pretty easy one. See this? You've got two pieces of bone where there should be one. Definitely broken."

Ian groans, glaring down at his thumb. "I thought you were going to have good news for me, Doc."

The lights come back on and she bats her eyes at him, pulling his hand into her own again.

"The good news is now you get to experience my magical healing fingers," she says, wiggling them for effect.

The urge to roll my eyes at her is *strong*. She's not subtle at all, and I thought there were rules about this sort of thing, doctors and patients and all that. Maybe it doesn't apply in a small town when options are limited.

"Why do I get the feeling that this is going to hurt?" Ian says. I wanted him to be nice but not this nice. Damn me. He's practically flirting with her at this point and I don't know if it's because I told him to play nice or because he's really responding to her tactics. But he did say she's not his type, so I've got that going for me. I take a deep breath and Ian glances at me.

"Only a little," she says, snapping a pair of gloves on. "Then it'll feel *so* much better."

I nearly gag. If she doesn't pump the brakes soon I might have to find a hose to turn on her.

But once Dr. Barnes gets to work setting his thumb, she's all business. Ian tries to crack a couple of jokes when he inadvertently shows how much pain he's in, but she's in serious doctor mode and not amused. It gives me way more faith in her abilities as a physician.

Once it's all wrapped up, she takes her gloves off, washes her hands, and turns to give Ian a stern look.

"Okay, now you need to be careful with that, okay? Take it easy."

"Sure thing, Doc," Ian agrees, but it's clear that he's just ready to get out of this office. I'm sure he's dealt with a lot of injuries throughout the years being a pro athlete, but I doubt you can ever really get used to people poking and prodding your injuries. And with broken bones like this, a lot of times the remedy is almost worse than the thing that caused it in the first place.

"I mean it," she says, wagging a finger at him.

Ian hops down off the table and chuckles, but I hear the agitation just below the surface. If she doesn't get out of his way soon, he might push by her. "You got it."

"You shouldn't even cook dinner. You should let me take you to Sheryl's instead."

I can see his shoulders stiffen, then he shakes his head. "Thanks, but no thanks. I can't, but I appreciate the offer."

Dr. Barnes frowns, but I don't really feel bad for her. She's trying too hard. Not to mention moving in on the guy *I'm* interested in. That's obviously her biggest crime.

"Right. Well, you should be fine to remove the soft cast in a few weeks. Just come in before you do and we'll do another x-ray to make sure it's completely healed."

He nods. "Thanks a lot."

She steps aside and Ian hurries out, me quick on his heels. He hands the receptionist his insurance card, but doesn't take the prescription for pain medicine the doctor wrote him.

"Seen too many of my friends get hooked on the stuff. I'd rather just be in pain," he tells me when I give him a look about it.

"Besides, if I were taking those pills, I couldn't drive. And even one-handed I'm not a total waste of space. I would be, on the drugs."

"Okay, okay, you win. You can handle the pain, Superman."

"I'm not trying to be macho or anything."

I grin. "But it's an added benefit, right?"

He gives me a sheepish look and a shrug. "All right, fine. You got me. So what?"

I laugh as he pulls the truck out of the parking lot. But I look back at the clinic and think about Dr. Barnes again.

Is it just her that Ian's not interested in, or is it all women?

I have to know.

It's driving me crazy.

"You should probably take some time off from working at

the camp with that," I say, trying to force my mind from the issue.

He frowns, grumbling something under his breath. "Maybe today. But I want to get back to work. You might have to deal with all the hard stuff for the next couple of weeks though."

Jesus, everything the man says is an innuendo, I swear. My face flames and the image of a very particular *hard thing* pops to mind. Me, sinking down to my knees, taking him in my mouth, leaving him helpless and at my mercy as I draw every last bit of pleasure out of him.

I can't keep not knowing. I just can't.

"Are you gay or straight?" I blurt out without even thinking about it. Immediately I'm mortified, clapping my hands over my mouth, my eyes wide with horror. "I'm so sorry, I shouldn't have asked that, that's totally your—"

"I'm gay," he says, his voice serious. "And I'm looking for a good man."

The way he says it... I swear there's something significant there. Something meaningful. But I don't have the courage to pursue it right now. Enough has already happened for one day and having an answer to that question is enough new information to deal with.

I don't say anything else the whole rest of the way to camp. Ian doesn't either. I don't know what it is, but he seems a little... uncertain now. It makes me frown, but I decide it's something to deal with another day.

"I'll see you tomorrow," I call as I jog over to my car. "And I'll bring you a real lunch!"

There's something about being with Ian that makes me restless. And hot. And bothered and itchy under my skin in a way that only one thing can fix. And I know it's crazy and impulsive and reckless, but I also know that images of Ian naked, his cock filling me, his cum shooting down my throat, aren't going anywhere if I don't deal with the throbbing problem in my pants.

I'm halfway home when I finally pull over to masturbate, thinking of Ian the whole time. And even though I come so hard I see spots in front of my eyes, it's not enough. It's not satisfying. Because now I know the truth. I know Ian's into men. I know I have a chance. And that's just about the hottest thing ever.

IAN

I spend the whole night tossing and turning in my tent. And I'd like to say that it's the hard ground under me, that it's my throbbing thumb, or even the unseasonably warm nighttime temperatures that keep me awake.

But it's none of those things.

The thing keeping me awake, keeping me tossing and turning and wishing I were somewhere else is Grant.

Well, okay, not Grant *exactly*.

I guess it's only tangentially related to Grant.

The thing that's keeping me up, more specifically, is *sex*.

I tell myself that it's just because it's been a while. Because I haven't been with anyone since I left the team.

Well, since they found out I'm gay. Because that opened a whole can of worms I never anticipated. The team finding out about my sexuality flipped my whole life upside down and really showed me what was important.

And I'll tell you a secret: that lesson wasn't that sex is what's important.

Not at all.

But that's what's consuming my brain. The idea of

sinking deep inside of someone, feeling them clench around me, my cock gripped by their muscles...

Let's be honest, it's not just *someone* I'm imagining. It's Grant. The way he fussed over me when I hurt myself, the way he insisted I go to the doctor and how he hovered over me the whole time we were there—I never would have put up with it from anyone else, but from him I *liked* it. I liked being fussed over and cared for and the center of his attention.

If any other guy treated me the way Grant did I'd be pissed, maybe even threatened by it, but with him I know it's from a place of caring. And I know it's because we're practically family already.

And even though that thought should discourage me from thinking about Grant stripping under the moonlight and beckoning me to bed, it doesn't. Clearly.

I keep thinking about the ride back to camp when he suddenly asked if I was gay. I can't believe Trevor never told him, but I guess my friend decided it wasn't his story to tell.

Still, the question's got me wondering. Because I know from Trevor that Grant is gay too. And I've seen the way he looks at me.

Is he feeling the same conflicting feelings I am? The pull that keeps trying to bring us together even though we both should know better?

Did Trevor warn him off of me?

If I were Trevor, I certainly would. I don't have the best reputation when it comes to relationships. Especially as far as Trevor's concerned.

We're guys. We talk about our conquests. Being gay doesn't change that, but now that I'm interested in his little brother I'm cursing myself for telling him all the sordid details all these years. He knows exactly how I pick up guys, use them for quick and dirty sex, and discard them.

Of course, that was when I was still in the closet for the sake of my career. Things are different now. Grant is different.

But try telling that to a protective older brother.

Still, no matter what I do, the thought of Grant dropping to his knees, gripping my cock, stroking me, looking up at me with those clear blue eyes as he swallows every inch of my throbbing erection keeps popping up in my head. Over and over again. Until I'm rock hard and my balls are *aching* from the lack of attention.

I've got to do something about this. I can't just stay up all night fantasizing or I'll be a zombie tomorrow and never get anything done.

"Cold shower it is," I mutter to no one in particular. It could be a hot shower now that I've got the plumbing hooked up and there's a solar water heater, but I think a cold one is going to serve me better.

Maybe I just have to shock the thoughts of Grant out of my head. Maybe if I make the water cold enough, my dick will just retreat into my body entirely and stop being such a persistent pain in the ass.

I grab a flashlight and crawl out of the tent, heading for the cabin that still doesn't have any electricity. Dark showers in the middle of the night, in a cabin in the woods, might freak some people out. But I don't have any room in my head to be freaked out. There's one thing and one thing only on my mind. And it's got nothing to do with being scared. Especially not with the way moonlight seems to be lighting the way straight to the cabin.

In the bathroom, I prop the flashlight up on the back of the toilet, but the weird cast of light it creates is almost worse than the pure dark. I don't actually need to see to wash or anything, I'm just planning on standing in the water, trying to cool my blood, so I switch the light off before closing the curtain.

The water's warm at first, and I slowly ease it into the cold side, my pores closing up, my skin tightening, goosebumps popping up all up and down my body.

But even as I try to rub the shivers out of my arms, I'm thinking of Grant here with me, Grant touching me tentatively, innocent with the way he looks up at me.

I don't know his history, but I have a pretty good guess. I've known guys like Grant before. The ones that are recently out and have fooled around with a couple of guys but never gotten serious. At least I don't think he's gotten serious with anyone.

My hand clenches into a fist at the very thought of Grant with another man. No. *Mine*.

The thought appears in my head from nowhere. It's strange, it's new and unusual, but it doesn't feel *wrong*. In fact, it feels very, very *right*. Making Grant mine in every way possible just sounds so right. I don't know how to stop wanting it, when even admitting it could mean losing my best friend.

Despite the freezing water, my cock is rock hard thinking about Grant. Every trickle of water down my body is his fingertips lightly touching me in the darkness. I imagine his lips working down my body, his tongue dragging down my shaft, teasing my balls. I imagine him opening his mouth so wide to take me in, filling his mouth so full that he's gagging, tears running down his face as I fuck his mouth.

I imagine Grant reaching down to touch himself as he sucks me off, watching his dick leak with precum because of how turned on he is by me using him like that.

Fuck. I groan, wrapping my hand around my pulsing cock. There's no avoiding it. There's no denying it. And if I don't touch myself soon, I might damn well be the first recorded fatal case of blue balls.

I hear Grant saying "I want you to fuck me, Ian," and it's damn near enough to make me explode. I wonder if Grant does dirty talk. I sure hope so. Hearing his perfect little mouth say something so filthy is something I'm not sure I can go on without hearing now that I've thought about it.

Grant is like that in a lot of ways. Once I think about him doing something, it's all-consuming. It's impossible to stop thinking about.

I move my hand faster and faster, sweating under the stream of water even though it should be freezing. My balls tighten up and my blood roars hot like lava in my veins. In my imagination, Grant pulls back right before I come and smiles at me. He knows he's got me right where he wants me and he blinks, innocent as you please.

"I want your cum on my face," imaginary Grant says and I roar as my orgasm *rips* through me, hot sticky ropes of cum splashing against the shower walls instead of Grant's perfect face.

My skin is still buzzing, my heart still racing when I turn the shower off and just lean against the wall, the cool tiles a comfort against my forehead.

What the hell is wrong with me?

I just jacked off to the thought of my *best friend's little brother*. That's cardinal sin territory. That's "I fuck up your face and forget about our twenty-year friendship" kind of territory.

And I wouldn't even really blame Trevor for feeling that way.

I look at my phone as I head back out to the tent. The Universe must be laughing at me. I've got a text from Trevor.

Barb's for drinks?

Shit. I feel like the worst friend in the world. I feel like I betrayed my buddy. All over jacking it.

But it's not just jacking it and I know it. What you're thinking about *in the moment* can say a lot about where a guy's head is at. It's why girls get so mad when they find out their men are jerking it to the thought of other women. And why Trevor would kick my ass if he got a glimpse of me right now.

He wouldn't even need to know what I did to know that he should kick my ass, because I know my guilt's written all over my face.

At least out here by the lake there's no one to see it. No one to witness my guilt and shame.

Not tonight, I text back. If he gives me any grief, I'll mention the broken thumb. That seems a good enough excuse to stay at home and be a grump.

Even if it's not my excuse at all. Even if my excuse is that I just want to sit in my tent and be grouchy knowing I can't have the thing I want most.

Or is it that I want him so much because I know I can't have him? It's hard to say, because before I came back to Umberland, I hadn't ever really given Grant a second thought. He's always been a kid. And not just any kid. My friend's kid brother.

Now he's still that, but he's also all grown up. And there's no denying that he's an adult now. Which is good, because my thoughts about him are *very* adult. Very adult and very dangerous.

Trevor might not be the most perceptive guy in the world, but he's bound to notice something eventually if something happens between Grant and me.

Even if it doesn't, when I'm hung up and thinking about someone, he's going to know. I just know he will. We're close like that. Best friends can always figure your shit out, even if you can't. Even when you wish they wouldn't.

And as much as I want to hate him for standing in my way, I can't. He's being a big brother. He's protecting his sibling. I imagine if I had any I'd do the same thing. Hell, I'm just over here fantasizing about Grant and I already want to protect him. I definitely can't blame Trevor.

Trevor isn't even the real reason I can't go after Grant. As much as I want to, as much as I feel like there's some invisible draw pulling us together wherever we go, I can't go after him because it wouldn't be right. Because he's young. And he's inexperienced. And I'd just end up hurting him.

I don't know how to do serious. I don't know how to do relationships. I rarely do more than a booty call and even the recurring friends with benefits I've had in the past didn't inspire me to learn things like their names or hobbies.

With Grant, it's different. I want to know everything and make his life perfect. The shitty thing is, I'm pretty sure his life would be a lot better without me in it. Without the drama and headaches that come with associating with me.

Not to mention his dreams of going off to the city, a place I can't ever see myself going back to after everything that happened there.

No, Grant and I are not meant to be. As strong as the attraction is between us, it needs to stay only that.

Finally, having decided that, I get a little bit of peace at not being so conflicted anymore. Even though I don't like the decision, I've finally made one and that's enough to soothe me a bit. I know my resolve's going to be tested—probably even before I wake up—but I'm a stubborn bastard and when I make up my mind, it's made up. I feel better having a resolution in place, even if the uneasy feeling in my stomach is screaming that it's wrong, and I'm finally able to turn over in my sleeping bag and fall asleep.

I still sleep like shit.

GRANT

"Look who finally decided to join us," Dad says as I come down the stairs into the kitchen. He's standing at the stove, cooking up bacon, and on the table there's already eggs and fried potatoes, toast, and juice.

"Mom already at the diner?" I ask, grabbing a glass and filling it with juice. If I go straight for coffee, Dad's bound to give me shit for it.

He nods and May pulls out a chair at the table. Back when we were younger, all of the Rainier kids from both families came here every morning for breakfast before school, after all our chores on the respective family farms. These days, we're a little more spread out, time obligations a little more demanding. But whenever someone's able, they're going to be at this table for breakfast. It's just the way we do things in our family.

"Come sit next to me," she says, patting the seat. "We still haven't had a chance to catch up." Trevor's sitting across from the empty seat and he gestures to it too.

I start piling my plate with food and shrug. "There's not a

lot to catch up on. I finished college and I'm back in town until I find a job in the city."

Scout huffs. "You need to stop saying that so loud. I swear Mom has a breakdown every time you remind her."

I roll my eyes. "She's just being dramatic. She didn't act like that with any of the rest of you."

"Yeah, but you're her *baby*," Trevor jeers, slathering a piece of toast with blackberry jam.

"I'm Dad's baby too, and he doesn't care what I do with my life, isn't that right, Dad?"

He grumbles and brings a plate of bacon to the table as he sits down. "Don't give your mom grief about loving you. Not everyone's got a mom to do that. Be grateful for what you've got."

I sigh and give up on waiting for coffee. I know he's got a point, but that doesn't mean I like it. I know I'm the baby, but it's not like I got a say in the matter. It's not like I got to choose to be coddled and fussed over my whole life, kept from doing anything that could be deemed too dangerous, left behind by my older siblings because I couldn't keep up.

Now that I'm finally an adult, finally able to move on and find my place in the world without always being the *baby*, Mom can't deal with it.

I'm sorry, but that's just not my problem. I'm here long enough for her to come to grips with it, but I'm not going to let anyone guilt me about leaving. It's my life, damn it.

"How's Aunt Aislynn?" I ask May, changing the subject as I sit back at the table with my coffee. Let her talk about *her* mom for a little while.

She sighs, rolling her eyes. "Oh, you know, wishing Dad would take her on trips and stuff but he's too busy with work, the usual."

"Must be glad Mom's not like that, eh Dad?" Scout teases. Trevor nearly chokes on his eggs trying to suppress a laugh and that makes May nearly lose it too. Dad's the only one with a straight face and he's looking downright grumpy.

He scoffs. "You think it's me that doesn't want to go anywhere? Our honeymoon was such a disaster that she swore off ever leaving Umberland again."

My eyebrows go up. "I thought Mom always said you guys didn't have a honeymoon."

"And if you ever talk to her about it, we didn't," Dad says plainly.

"Understood," says May solemnly. Then she turns on me, flashing that thousand-watt smile of hers.

"What have you been up to since you've been back in town?"

I shrug. "Little of this little of that, nothing too exciting."

"Don't be modest," Scout says, prodding me under the table with her foot. "You've got that job helping fix up Camp Eagle Peak."

"Oh?" May asks, her eyebrows raised as she stabs some potatoes.

"With *Ian*," Scout adds, making a point to emphasize his name.

May gasps. "No way. No. Way. Seriously?"

Scout just grins and nods. Trevor's brow furrows and he looks over at me like something's just clicking for him.

"What are you guys—" Dad and I are wearing the same confused frown, but it's me that tries to talk to them.

"You mean Ian like the guy Grant's always had a crush on, Ian?" May asks, grinning from ear to ear.

Shit. How did they know? Leave it to my cousin and my sister to tease me about a crush I had when I was a kid. Never mind that it's a crush I *still* have.

"Wait… you knew I was gay? I didn't think anyone knew until I came out a few months ago."

Scout snorts into her glass of milk, making bubbles go up over her nose.

"Jeez, Grant, what do you take us all for, idiots? Of course we knew you were gay. We all knew. Not that we cared, obviously."

I sigh. I guess I really can't keep any secrets from my family. It's ridiculous.

"But don't change the subject," May says in a sing-song voice. "Tell me about working with *Iiiiaaan.*"

"You guys… It's not… We're not… I don't…" The more I try to argue, the more they're making knowing faces at me and grinning and nodding and making me feel flustered and cornered.

"You should stay away from him," Trevor says, gruff and grumbly.

"Oh? And why is that?" I can't help myself. I'm tired of other people thinking they get a say in what I choose to do with my life. Especially Trevor and his overbearing ways. I know I'm just making everything worse by being snippy about them teasing me, and I know that's just going to make me more suspicious, but damn it, I'm sick of this.

"Because he's too old for you," Trevor says. Then, like he's realizing that's a really crappy reason to not date someone—especially when the age difference is in single digits—he's quick to add, "Besides, he's my best friend. That would be really weird for me."

I roll my eyes, scoffing. "I'll be sure to structure my love life around what's comfortable for you," I say.

He grins, knowing I'm giving him shit, but being a pain in the ass older brother anyway. "'Preciate it."

"I don't remember you ever having a rule to protect *us* from feeling uncomfortable," Scout says, wrinkling her nose. "That guy you dated right after high school was…" She exaggerates a shudder.

"Way too old for you," Dad grumbles, finishing her sentence for her.

"He wasn't *that* much older. Maybe six years," Trevor says defensively.

"Ian's only eight years older than me," I point out, though I know I'm not helping my case if I want them to believe I'm not still into him.

"He's still my best friend," Trevor says.

"Wonder how you even have any of those," I snap back.

May gives a surprised giggle-snort into her orange juice and Dad looks completely exasperated with all of us.

"Don't any of you have work to be doing?" he grumbles, already finishing his breakfast even though he was the last to join the table.

Trevor pushes back from the table and takes his dishes to the sink too. "You know I do, Pop."

Dad claps him on the back. "Just don't work yourself too hard. Make sure you leave time for what's important."

It's a surprisingly genuine thing for Dad to say and I can't help but wonder if there's something going on with Trevor I don't know about. We've never been all that close—the age difference made sure of that—but his proclivity for being a jerk didn't really help either.

Still, he's my big brother, and if something's going on in his life, I feel like I should know about it.

Shouldn't I?

May and I get up and wash the dishes as Scout puts everything away and hurries out to do her own stuff. We make quick work of cleaning up and we're both heading out the front door to our respective cars.

"So," May says, casually, but with a hint of something that makes me uneasy. "*Are* you still crushing on Ian?" She smirks, eying me carefully.

"That was a long time ago, May. I was just a kid with a silly kid crush."

She grins, her eyes sparkling with mischief.

"So that's a yes, then?"

I start to stammer and protest, but she doesn't really give me the chance.

"Well, good luck," she says. "And ignore Trevor. How he feels about it doesn't really matter."

"I plan to," I say, basically admitting outright my desire for Ian. Guess there really aren't any secrets in this family.

The whole way to the camp I'm thinking about breakfast and how Trevor tried to warn me off of his friend. Is it really just their friendship and the age difference that makes him think I shouldn't pursue anything with Ian?

Trevor arguably knows him better than most people. If he thinks I shouldn't…

I shake my head, tightening my hands on the wheel. May's right. I need to just ignore what he says.

I'm driving up through the woods and I pass a little pull-off on the road. Not just any pull-off, but the same place I stopped my car yesterday to jerk off while thinking about Ian. The memory comes flooding back and my face is bright red and hot in an instant.

I can't believe I did that! And now I'm going to be awkward around him every time I look at him, thinking about the fantasies from yesterday. I curse myself, but I just have to suck it up and deal with it.

The camp comes into view and I see Ian's truck and his tent, but the flap's open, so I know he's probably already up and doing things.

My tires crunching on the gravel doesn't coax him out, so I go looking. I find him in the main cabin trying to rip up old yellowed linoleum with his one good hand.

"Hey," I say, getting down on my hands and knees to help.

"Hey," he answers, grunting as a strip of the linoleum rips free.

"How's your thumb?" I ask, ripping up a good hunk of the floor.

"Getting in my way," he grumbles, sweat already starting to drip down the side of his forehead. He looks like he had a rough night. There are bags under his eyes and they're a little bloodshot, and he's got that kind of pale, almost sick look of someone that's running on empty.

"Thought I was supposed to handle all the hard work," I say, trying to muscle my way in.

He shouldn't be working with that broken thumb. He's just going to injure himself worse. Besides, as long as he's working and grunting next to me, I'm going to have to fight off an uncomfortably inappropriate erection. He just looks so damn good hard at work, with sweat dripping down the chiseled planes of his face, his sharp jaw highlighted by the rough stubble of a few days without shaving, his eyes narrowed with a determination that makes my brain run amok with possibilities. I can't handle it and it's too damn early in the morning to try.

He grumbles something, but backs off, leaving the cabin and me alone to rip up the linoleum.

Great.

Guess I got what I wanted.

A minute later I hear the whir of the saw coming to life and know there's no more talking happening for a while.

But that suits me just fine. With Ian out of the house and a demanding task at hand, I'm able to stop thinking about yesterday and how turned on I got. But every time I hear the roar of the saw stop, I wonder if he's coming back in and I hope, holding my breath until it starts up again and I'm disappointed.

Until the time that it doesn't start up again, and instead

the door swings open and Ian comes in, glistening, lit from behind like some kind of Greek god.

"How's it goin'?"

I shrug. "Almost got everything ripped up."

He nods and walks around, giving me a wide berth like he's afraid he's going to catch some disease or something from me. He's not really looking at me either. He's avoiding coming near me, avoiding looking at me…

Shit. What did I do? Was it because I asked if he was gay? Am I just giving off weird vibes because of how awkward I feel now? I don't know what it is, but Ian's definitely being weird too.

"Ready to lay the new floor?" he asks.

"Got wood for me?" I ask, realizing too late what I just said.

Ian cracks a smile. "More than you can handle."

Even though my face is *burning* and I can't believe I'm basically flirting with him, I say, "Try me. I might surprise you."

His eyebrows go up, but he doesn't challenge me. He just jerks his head back toward the door.

"Come on, help me bring this stuff inside."

IAN

For a couple of hours Grant and I work on the floors. It's hard work with only one hand, and he doesn't make it any easier fussing over me every few minutes.

"What are you doing? Give me that," he says, snatching away the rubber mallet in my hand before I can knock the floorboard into place.

"This job is going to take ten times as long if you don't let me help. I have nine other fingers."

He gives me a look and I grin. I know I'm making this difficult for him, but I think he likes it. I think he likes that I'm incorrigible. That I make him blush with every other sentence.

I know *I* like it.

As much as I try not to. As much as I try to remind myself that last night I swore I wasn't going to do anything with Grant, I wasn't going to pursue my best friend's little brother, and I was going to do my damnedest to forget all the inappropriate thoughts I had about the youngest Rainier.

But none of that is working. Because no matter how

many promises I made to myself last night, today's a new day, and today, I don't give a shit about the resolutions I thought were so important last night.

Today Grant's here in front of me, reminding me every minute why I can't just walk away and forget about him.

"It's going to take even longer if we keep having to have this argument. You injuring yourself again and us spending *another* day in Dr. Barnes's office isn't going to help the timeline either."

I huff. "Did Trevor put up with this kind of bossiness when you worked for him?"

He stops, his shoulders stiffening, and I wonder if maybe I've taken it too far. Maybe that was the wrong thing to say, to remind him that he's working for me, to bring up his brother. I know I just killed the easy flirty thing we've had going on all day.

Then his shoulders relax a bit and he looks over one of them at me, still on the floor on his hands and knees. He smiles, and seeing him in that position sends a bolt of lightning straight to my dick. I try to memorize the sight for later and instantly feel guilty about it.

I shouldn't be planning on thinking about Grant later, cock in hand. I know I shouldn't. But it was *so good* last night, even if I wanted more. Even if I still do. I know better than to hope for that, so is there really any harm in putting one in the spank bank?

"No, but if he did, his jobs would've gotten done faster," he says, a spark of sass in his tone that I don't think I've heard before. I can hardly stand it.

He wants me to just stand back here and watch him work. Watch him on his hands and knees on the ground, his ass up in the air for me, his grunts and groans of exertion filling the cabin. I'm supposed to just stand here and endure that. What did I do to deserve such punishment?

"Why don't we have lunch?" I ask. It's about the right time for it and I don't really want to bicker about whether or not I should be permitted to do work on my own property. And I don't want to just stand here watching Grant. That's getting dangerous enough as it is. If it goes on for much longer, I don't know if my will power will hold. And then who knows what kind of mess I'll make.

He sits back on his heels and wipes sweat from his brow, looking even more vibrant and youthful with the flush of hard work in his cheeks. He looks at me as if considering it for a moment before letting out a breath and nodding.

"Yeah, okay. I brought you a sandwich today so you're not stuck eating trail mix."

"What's wrong with trail mix? Protein keeps you fueled throughout the day."

"Nothing's wrong with trail mix if you're hiking or under the age of three. Grown men shouldn't be eating it for meals."

I grin, shoving my good hand in my pocket, rocking on my heels. "You know, you sound an awful lot like your mom right now."

I brace myself for him to hit me—hell, I'd deserve it, I just love pressing his buttons—but it doesn't happen. He glowers at me instead.

"You shouldn't say things like that to the person that's feeding you. That's how you get poisoned."

I laugh and follow him out of the cabin as he heads to his car for his insulated lunch box.

"There are worse people to be compared to. You shouldn't threaten to poison me if you really want me to eat something other than my trail mix. Besides, it's been serving me all right out here when it's too hot to cook and I don't wanna go down to your mom's diner."

He's still giving me a hard look as he plops a sandwich in

my hand. "Next time you're tempted to eat trail mix for dinner, let me know and I'll bring you real food."

"Is that a promise?" I ask, injecting more suggestion into it than I probably should. He tries to hide it in a shrug, but I see his flush and feel a little bit of satisfaction at it.

"Why don't we go eat by the lake? It's such a nice day," I say, heading off down the gently sloping path, assuming he'll follow.

But when I get to the dock, I turn to say something to him, and Grant's not behind me. Instead, he's up on the shore at an old rickety picnic table, gingerly taking a seat.

Not quite what I meant, but okay. If he wants to sit there, we'll sit there.

I head up to the picnic table too, and hold my breath as I sit down on the ramshackle pile of wood. I'm surprised it holds both of us, but I'm not going to trust it to reliably do it.

"We should make it a priority to get this fixed up next so we have somewhere to have lunch," I say, pulling my sandwich out. "Unless you'd rather sit on the dock with our feet in the water?"

That's what I'd been imagining when I suggested eating by the lake. Us on the dock, the sun in our faces, our toes in the water… Laughing… Splashing… Kissing…

Maybe the picnic table is a better choice.

"This is good," Grant says like he's reading my mind. But it's not just that he's reading my mind. There's something else there, something I feel like I should know even though I can't seem to put my finger on it.

"Is everything okay?"

He nods quickly. "Yeah. I just… I don't like that lake. Or water at all really. Not after…"

It all comes rushing back to me. Grant much, much younger, trying to swim too far out in the lake, getting pulled under by the wake of a boat, thrashing, having trouble surfacing, being carted to shore by the lifeguard on duty.

How could I have forgotten?

"Not since you almost drowned," I say, putting it all together.

"Not the most successful attempt at learning to swim there ever was," he says ruefully, staring out at the lake like it's an old archenemy.

But I catch what he's not saying outright.

"You're telling me you don't know how to swim? You never tried again?"

He scoffs. "After that disastrous first attempt? Hell no."

"You can't just be afraid forever, Grant. You can't let your fear control you. What if someone you cared about needed help? What if you were on a cruise ship that was sinking?"

"A cruise isn't very high on the list of things I want to do with my time," he says.

I sigh. "Come on. Let me teach you. I'll be gentle. I'll go slow."

He puts his sandwich down and looks at me across the table that creaks with every movement. "You're not going to drop this until I agree, are you?"

I grin. "Nope."

He sighs, shaking his head. "Why? Have I been a bad employee? Do you *want* to hurt me?"

"Oh, come on. There are worse things than skipping work on a hot summer afternoon to go swimming," I tease, nudging him under the table with my foot.

"Fine," he groans. "You win."

I just smile at him, and for the next few minutes while we're finishing up our sandwiches, I don't say anything more about it.

"The floor's going down good," he says. "We should be able to finish it in another day or two."

I nod. "Yeah. I'll probably just move in at that point. Anything else that pops up can wait until other stuff around camp's been addressed."

"I bet you'll be happy to have a real place to sleep again," he says. "It can't be fun to be in a sleeping bag in a tent long-term."

"It's not great, but it's okay," I say, shrugging. I want to say something about it not mattering *where* you sleep, but rather who's there with you, but it sounds ridiculously cheesy even in my head so I don't.

"I had a semester in college where I basically had to sleep on the wooden couches in the common room because my roommate was always bringing people home... Even that was terrible. I woke up walking funny every day."

"Not normally why people are walking funny," I say, grinning. He chuckles too, nodding.

"I know. I'd have much preferred the other reason, not that there was any danger of *that* happening..." He presses his lips together as soon as he says it, but it's enough to confirm my suspicions that Grant's inexperienced.

"Come on, let's go," I say, standing from the picnic table, holding my hand out to support it as I do. I pull my shirt up over my head and when I look at Grant again, he's looking at me like I've lost my mind.

"What are you doing?"

"It's time for your swimming lesson," I say.

"*Now?*"

I grin. "Would you rather go back to work?"

"But... but... aren't you supposed to wait an hour after eating?"

"Oh come on, now. That's an old wives' tale."

His eyes dart back to the path that leads to the cabin, and I swear he's considering running up it, but finally he gives up the fight.

"I don't have swim trunks," he says weakly.

"Me neither," I say, pulling my shorts, socks, and shoes off, standing there in nothing but my boxers. Grant's staring at me, and I'm sure at least part of it is pure shock at what I'm suggesting, but I'm also sure that another part of it is him plain checking me out.

The cold water laps at my feet as I back up to the water's edge, my arms outstretched toward the shore.

"Come on out, the water's fine," I call. It's a lie. It's freezing out here, still a little early in the season to be swimming in the lake, but I'm not passing up my opportunity right now. I see a chance to get closer to Grant and I'm going to take it.

"You're serious about this?" he asks, still eying me closely as I back farther into the lake, cold water all the way up to my waist now. My dick and balls start to shrivel up and retract inside of me at the shock of cold, but I just ignore it—and the goosebumps—and before too long I've adjusted to the chill.

He looks uncertain as he pulls his shirt up over his head, but I'm not complaining about how slow he's going. The look of him stripping is so hot, I wonder if I might steam up the frigid lake. I get to watch as inch after inch of his freckled skin is revealed, his lean muscles—natural from work, not from hours in the gym—stretching as he wrestles the fabric over his head. His shoes are next, then his socks. He takes them off slowly and folds them together, tucking them in one of his shoes.

"You're stalling," I call, wafting my arms to move around in the water.

"Of course I am! This is a crazy idea."

"And if you don't hurry up, I'm going to pull you in here." His eyes go wide and panicked, but I hold out my hands to let him know I'm not serious. I'd never do that. Maybe if he were a great swimmer and we'd played around like that before, but not with him being scared and not knowing how to swim. I want to teach him and help him, not torture him.

Finally, he unbuttons his shorts and lets them fall to the ground in a pile with his shoes and shirt. The look's not all that different since he's wearing boxers too, but it *feels* different. It feels intimate, maybe only because I want it to, but it does.

I wade closer to the shore as Grant takes a step into the water, then another. He's hugging himself, shaking like a leaf by the time just his ankles are submerged. It could be cold or it could be terror.

"It's c-c-c-cold," he says, teeth chattering.

"You've gotta get farther in," I say gently, now close enough to grab him if I need to. Nothing's going to happen to him while I'm around.

He shakes his head and I can see how scared he is. This was meant to be flirty fun, but quickly I see this is a real mountain for Grant to climb. I want to be his climbing guide. I want to help him scale this hurdle.

All thoughts of sex go out the window—okay, not *all,* but I'm a red-blooded male and he's too damn cute not to want— and I just focus on Grant and making sure he's doing okay.

"I've got you," I promise, reaching my hand out to him. "Nothing's going to happen while I'm here."

His teeth rake over his bottom lip, and he looks from my eyes down to my palm and back again. His hand slides into mine and he clings so tight I think he might break my other fingers, but I don't even care. It's worth it.

He takes a shaky step forward without me prompting. Then another. Every time he takes a step forward, I take one backward to match him, still holding his hand, still right there if he needs me.

And before either of us knows it, he's up to his waist in

water. Of course, it's not easy for him. He's breathing fast and shallow, his cheeks flushed, his eyes wide, looking up at me. It's a look I've seen so many times, but usually it's desire, not fear. Usually it's a good look.

His eyes dart around, finding water on all sides, and I see the rational part of his brain getting shoved aside by panic. I can see it happening and I know I need to stop it before he gives up on ever trying this again.

So I do the only thing I can think to do.

I kiss him.

It's almost an unconscious instinct with the way he's looking like he's in the throes of desire. It's almost like he's beckoning me to kiss him. But beyond that, I know he's panicking because he's thinking too much and I know this is one surefire way to stop it.

Sure enough, he freezes for just a moment, and I let my lips linger on his, letting him realize what's happening before I start to move again, sucking on his bottom lip gently. His breath hitches and it makes something inside of me snap. It's too hard just to be gentle with him. I can't just take this slow because it's Grant and I'm desperate for *everything, right now.*

I force myself to go slow, to let him deepen the kiss on his own terms.

Apparently, Grant's just as hungry for it as I am. A moan forms in the back of his throat as my tongue slips into his mouth and he tilts his head back to let me in deeper.

Fuck, it's everything I imagined it would be and more. He's so soft and supple, so sweet and innocent, but so eager, so hungry... it's goddamn intoxicating. Irresistible.

And when we break apart, I actually groan. I never want to stop kissing him, even if I am out of breath. I want more and I want it now. He looks embarrassed, but there's no reason for it. I won't let him be.

I smile. "Should I do that any time you're scared of the water?"

He's breathless when he says, "Maybe." He's still clutching my hand, trying to catch his breath as he looks over his shoulder. "Can we go back to the shore now? I think I've spent enough time in the water for one day."

I chuckle and nod, squeezing his hand in mine. Everything about this moment is perfect and pure and I never want to forget it. I don't even want it to end. But I know asking Grant to stay in the water any longer would be mean.

He keeps hold of my hand the whole time he wades to shore, but once we're out of the water, he's quick to get dressed and pack up his lunch stuff. We head back to the cabin and go back to work without ever mentioning the kiss again.

But that doesn't mean I'm not thinking about it. I can't get the memory of Grant's lips on mine out of my head. The way he responded to me, how open he was and willing to give himself to me.

How the hell am I supposed to resist that?

I don't even want to.

And I'm not going to.

To hell with what Trevor says or thinks. Who cares if he doesn't approve?

I feel something with Grant. Something I haven't felt with anyone else before. And I'm not going to miss out on seeing what it is just because my best friend can't handle his little brother having a boyfriend. If he's really my friend, he'll just have to understand that.

GRANT

I'm trying to focus on my work laying floorboards, cutting them to fit around the corners, making sure everything's tight and secure. But I'm not having much success focusing because my mind keeps going back to the lake.

Instead of a wave of panic washing over me at the thought of the lake that traumatized me as a kid, it's a wave of something else flooding my body, warming my blood, making me itch with *want*. I think about Ian luring me out into the water, beckoning me with those clear blue-green eyes, telling me everything was all right.

And with him, I knew it was. I knew that he would never let anything happen to me. Don't ask me how I knew that, considering the way he and Trevor treated me when I was younger, but there's something different about how he acts around me now.

I know that Ian will protect me. I know he's looking out for me. I know that with him I'm safe and secure and I don't have to worry.

But I don't know if I'm reading too much into things.

I'm pretty sure that kiss was *something*. I mean, obviously it was a kiss, so it had to mean something, right? But what did it mean?

Clearly, it's an admission of attraction on both of our parts. There's no denying that. That makes me uncharacteristically bold. It makes me want to go out of my comfort zone and see how far I can push this.

Ian Barrett is into me, and I'm going to use that knowledge to my advantage in any way I can.

"Spiders are gonna be mad you're kicking them out," I say, brushing aside the dozenth cobweb of the day. There's nothing like an empty cabin in the woods to attract spiders from miles around, I swear.

"Yeah, but they'll get over it. It's retaliation from the teenagers losing their drinking spot that I'm more worried about."

I frown. I hadn't really considered that before, but he's got a point. A lot of teenagers act entitled to whatever they want and don't really care if it belongs to someone else. At least the kind of teenagers that are out in the woods drinking and graffitiing abandoned buildings.

"You've got Ryan's number, don't you?"

He looks confused. "Your cousin Ryan?"

"Yeah," I answer, confused about his confusion. We're both looking at each other trying to figure out what the other one's missing when it hits me. "Ryan's the sheriff now. I keep forgetting you've been out of the loop."

Understanding dawns on his expression and he nods. "His number would be great, thanks."

"Sure, can never be too careful."

He grins. "Careful's not really something I'm known to be, you know."

I look at his thumb pointedly. "I realize that. That's why you're lucky you have me around."

I almost wince as soon as I say it. Normal things I would never give a second thought to, normal playful things, sound so much more suggestive when I say them to Ian. It sounds like I'm practically throwing myself at him and I can't seem to stop. I don't know why, but my mouth seems to have a mind of its own.

Ian doesn't look put off by my brazen statement though. He just smiles as he hands me the next plank of wood. "Yeah, I am." The warm sincerity in his tone is enough to spawn a million butterflies in my stomach. It's now or never. If I don't try it now, I may never have the nerve to do it again.

"Do you wanna come to dinner at our house tonight?" I ask quickly. It shouldn't even be that strange of an invitation. Ian's been to dinner at our house a thousand times. But always as Trevor's guest. And never after kissing me in the lake.

As soon as I ask it, I'm sure he's going to shy away. I'm sure that I'm coming on too strong again and ruining whatever minor progress we've made, but it's done now and I'll just have to face the consequences.

"I'd love to," he says, quickly following it up with, "I never miss a chance to enjoy Sheryl's cooking. Especially for free," he adds with a wink.

I smile back at him, but the feeling in my chest is less than pleased. He's coming because he's basically already part of the family. It's not because he kissed me and I want to bring him home. It's just Ian, coming over like he has so many other times.

I don't know what I want to be different. I know I don't want the same old thing that's always happened. But what can I do? How can I stop being the annoying little kid that always tried to join their adventures and actually be seen as a sexual, desirable adult?

It's a few hours later when we finally call it quits for the day and I still haven't figured out a better plan for dealing with the Ian situation. I guess I'll just have to play it by ear.

"Do you want a ride?" I ask as I head to my car, nervousness finally bubbling up inside of me now that it's really happening. Now that the day's work is over and it's actually time for Ian to come over to my parents' house for dinner.

I've never brought a boy home before, and even now I'm not sure that's what I'm doing. Because I'm not really sure what's happening between us, if anything. I'm not even sure if Ian knows. But the point is, I don't know the protocol for things like this. I don't know what I'm supposed to do, how I'm supposed to act, if there are certain things I should say or I definitely *shouldn't* say. I just don't know. And not knowing makes me more nervous than anything else.

"Thanks, but I think I should probably take a shower before I come over if I want your mom to ever let me back in her house."

"Sounds good," I say, trying desperately not to think about him in the shower, naked, water cascading down his muscular body, steam coiling around him... Yeah, obviously I fail at trying not to think about it. It doesn't help that I have a template now after seeing him in his boxers at the lakeshore. It doesn't take much effort for my imagination to erase the last scraps of fabric from that memory, filling in the blanks with explicit images that would make a porn star blush. "See you in about an hour?" I manage, the words almost a squeak as they come out.

Ian smiles and nods. "It's a date," he says.

I jump in my car before I can react to that.

Is it a date? That's just a saying, right? But is it, in this case? Because...

I grumble and curse at myself as I pull away from the camp and head back to my parents' house. I'm not normally this wishy-washy. I don't normally second-guess myself this much. But with Ian I'm just not sure if anything I'm doing is right.

That's one thing they don't tell you when people encourage you to try new things. Everyone talks about how exciting and *fun* it is. No one talks about the crippling anxiety that you're doing everything wrong and making a fool of yourself.

But I can't be afraid forever. Even if nothing happens with Ian, I need to get over this fear if I ever want to have hope of dating in the future.

And I do. I want someone to share my life with. Maybe even raise a family with. I don't want to be alone forever. And part of making sure that doesn't happen is learning how to date, how to interact with guys I'm attracted to without making a complete and utter fool of myself.

When I get home, Mom is in the kitchen peeling vegetables and I take the detour through to give her a hug and a kiss on the side of the forehead.

"Hey, Mom."

"You stink," she says, wrinkling her nose and pulling away, but she's smiling and I know she's happy I'm here. Most of the time I am too, but I know it can't be that way forever. I know that Umberland just isn't big enough for the kind of dreams I have, and nothing's going to change that no matter how much I love my family.

"I'm heading up to the shower. I just wanted to let you know that I invited Ian to dinner. He's been up there in a tent trying to pass off jerky and nuts as a meal."

Mom looks as offended by that as I felt watching it. I knew she'd appreciate the severity of the issue.

"I'm glad you invited him then. I thought he knew better."

"Guess he's been away from you too long," I say grinning. "You'll have to whip him back into shape."

She's grinning to herself, but when she looks over at me

her look is more serious, like she's trying to figure something out.

"Grab me three more potatoes out of the cupboard, would you? There's never enough scalloped potatoes for that boy."

I chuckle and grab the potatoes, dropping them on the counter next to her cutting board.

"Anything else?"

"Not from you, stinky," she says, wrinkling her nose. "Go on, get out of here."

I'm not going to argue. It's not like I actually *want* to get roped into cutting and peeling vegetables. I just know if I don't at least offer to help that I'm going to hear about it later.

By the time I'm out of the shower and heading downstairs again, I can hear the whole family talking—well, not the *whole* family, it's only our side and Sawyer's not here, not that he ever is. And mixed in all those familiar voices, I hear another. I hear Ian laughing, his deep voice rumbling through the house even though I can't make out the words. The butterflies are back in full force and I almost stop at the bottom of the stairs and turn around again, getting cold feet, but Scout's onto me.

"Grant, is that you coming downstairs?" she calls.

"It's not the ghost," I answer, popping my head in the little dining room attached to the kitchen. I say little because it's not really its own room, but it's big enough to host our whole family. It's just the way old farmhouses were built and it suits Mom just fine.

"Take this," she says, waving a cell phone at me. "Put it by the door. This chucklehead thinks he can have his phone at the table."

"I'm pretty sure the last time I was here for dinner cell

phones weren't even really a thing yet," Ian argues in his defense.

"And whose fault is that? That whole fancy professional career and you couldn't even come back to visit your old hometown?" Mom says, laying the guilt on thick as she delivers steaming-hot dishes to the table.

"Well, he's back now, Mom. No need to send him to the gallows," Trevor argues.

"I know," she says apologetically. "But you all know how I am about my babies, and like it or not, Ian, you're one of my kids too."

Ian looks a little surprised by that, like he doesn't know what to say. It's weird, because to us that kind of statement is totally normal, but then I remember that Ian's an only child and his parents are dead. I realize how strange it must be to have that kind of affection coming at you from his point of view.

"How's the camp coming?" Trevor asks, flipping the topic effortlessly as we all start to pile our plates up high.

"It's coming," Ian says. "Slow going with this," he says holding up his casted thumb, "but Grant's been a godsend."

"What did you do to it?" Scout asks, frowning at his hand.

Ian shrugs. "Just bein' stupid and careless, nothing new."

"Oh man, remember that time we decided to try to catch balls bare-handed at the batting cages?" Trevor asks.

"You did what?" Dad grumbles.

Ian winces, flexing his injured hand. "My wrist still clicks." They both laugh about it and even though I'm not really in the conversation at all, I can't help but marvel at how well Ian's reintegrating with my family. It's like he never left at all. Like all the years are just melting away and we're back in old times. There's an easy air that wasn't there when I was a kid and certain topics had to be avoided to protect my little ears.

"You're lucky you didn't hurt yourself more seriously pulling dumb stunts like that," Mom says, jabbing a fork in the air at Trevor and Ian.

Trevor grins. "Mom, you'd have a heart attack if you knew the half of it."

She sighs and rolls her eyes, muttering a prayer under her breath. "I don't doubt it. But you could have lost out on that whole career of yours," she says to Ian.

"I know," he admits. "It was stupid. I've done a lot of really dumb things and been very lucky that they haven't had the consequences they could have."

"You know, I don't follow sports much, but I always kept an eye out for your name," Dad says, earning a surprised look from all of us. Dad's not much of a sports guy. He knows enough from playing when he was a kid, from helping Trevor and Sawyer with their little leagues, even being a coach when the town needed it, but I wouldn't say it's an *interest* of his. I'd never have pegged him as ever even *opening* the sports section.

"I really appreciate that, Mr. Rainier," Ian says, clearly humbled.

"But what I don't understand is why you quit. You were doing well, making a name for yourself, highest RBI in the division… Is there an injury that didn't get reported?"

I realize it's coming from a place of concern and love, but I see Ian tense up in an instant and can't help but remember the terse interaction we had in the truck on the way back from urgent care. I know baseball is one of the topics that Ian's touchy about, but I don't know how to let Dad know now that it's already too late.

"I… uh… Well, you know, I'm happy with the things I achieved in my career, but it just seemed like it was time for me to be doing something else with my life," he says, stammering through it at first before falling into something that sounds very forced and very rehearsed.

I frown, looking at Ian, but he's too busy not looking at anyone to notice. He's intently focused on his food, staring down at the plate without looking up.

Mom and Dad exchange a look and I can tell that they're having one of their silent conversations. With four nosy kids and five nieces and nephews that were just as bad, they've gotten pretty good at talking without saying anything.

"It'll be nice to have that old camp back up and running," Mom says, pivoting expertly. "It's been a hazard for years now. Just last fall some kids were out there playing and one fell through the floor of one of the cabins. His friends didn't want to get in trouble for playing where they shouldn't be, so they just left him there. Launched a full-scale search and rescue for the kid before one of his friends finally cracked and spilled the whole story."

"*That* explains that hole," Ian says, nodding at the revelation, earning some chuckles around the table.

The tense mood fades and easy conversation returns. There's a lot that Ian's missed in the last ten or so years, and Mom's eager to fill him in on every bit of gossip, even though I can see him getting bored of it pretty quickly. Everyone's done eating and we're just sitting around the table chatting when Mom finally pushes herself up from her seat.

"These dishes aren't going to wash themselves."

"Can I help?" Ian asks, standing quickly.

"That's all right, honey. I'll get one of my two-handed children to help out. Scout?"

Scout sighs and grumbles something about the boys never having to help, but no one pays her any attention.

"Come on," I say, jerking my head as I get up. I lead him out to the front porch and sit on the swing there, hoping he'll join me.

He does, and now I don't know what to say. I just know I invited him here because there were so many strange and confusing emotions swirling around after that kiss and I wanted to see if it meant anything. I wanted to see what would happen, but bringing him home, bringing him to *my* family, just meant that he pretty much talked to everyone but me all night.

And I love that Ian gets along with my family. It just makes him more attractive to me. But I'm also feeling a little left out, so it's nice to just sit here in silence with him, gently rocking on the porch swing.

"Thanks for inviting me tonight. I forgot how much I love it here."

I smile, laughing softly to myself. "I'm glad you came. I'm surprised you still love them after they prod and pry into your life."

He sighs, his shoulders tensing. "Yeah, but I know it's only because they care."

"That's true," I say, nodding. "Dad didn't mean anything asking about your retirement…"

"I know," he says, another heavy sigh leaving his lungs as he leans forward, his face crumpled with deep thought.

"You know… You don't have to and I totally understand if you don't want to, but if you ever *did* want to talk about it…"

Ian blows out another heavy breath and I think I've gone too far. I pushed too hard again and he's just going to shut down and close me out.

"I had a boyfriend visit me at an away game. I'd done it before. I was careful. But I got sloppy and a teammate saw him leaving my room. Saw us kissing in the doorway. He flipped out and spilled to the whole team. And even though no one came right out and said that was why, they suddenly started to make my life hell.

"The people I thought were my friends stood by and did

89

nothing. They didn't participate in making me feel unwelcome or all the little hazing things, but they didn't stand up for me either. They didn't want me there. And honestly, after all of that, I didn't want to be there anymore. They preach all this bullshit about how you're a team, how you're family, how you're there for each other. But they turned their backs on me because they didn't like that I'm gay."

His voice is shaking and mad, but he pauses to take a breath and lets it out slowly.

"I realized that everything and everyone I'd ever loved that wasn't part of baseball was in Umberland, so I came back."

He says that like it's the simplest solution to the nightmare he's been through. And I'm glad he thinks that. I'm glad that coming back was his answer, because now he's here with me.

I reach out and slowly take his hand, waiting for him to pull back, to reject me, but he doesn't. He holds my hand too, and we sit there on the porch swing rocking back and forth for a while. There aren't any words to make it better. I don't have anything to say to comfort him, but I hope through my hand I'm able to tell him how sorry I am for what he went though. How angry I am at those jerks for not being there for him. How much I want to make everything all better. To help him show those assholes he doesn't need them.

Right now I can't really say all that, but I think I get the message across sitting there holding his hand, trying to pour all those emotions into the gesture.

The front door creaks open and Ian and I immediately pull our hands apart. I don't know who let go first, but I'm immediately mad that our reaction has to be like that. Trevor comes out, spots us just quietly rocking on the porch swing, and gives us a suspicious look. I don't even care if he suspects anything. I don't care if he outright knows. I just want to make sure that Ian's okay with that first. I'm not scared of my brother's reaction, but I think Ian might bear the brunt of it, so I'm treading carefully for his sake.

"Mind if I join you?" he asks, scooting in between us without waiting for an answer.

Yeah, he definitely suspects something.

"I was talking to Caleb the other day," he says facing Ian. "He's definitely single and interested if you want his number."

"Uh, that's okay," Ian says, sending a look over Trevor's head to me.

"You sure?" Trevor asks. "You said you wanted to date, and there's not a lot of prospects around here. Caleb's kind of a catch. Though, I'm pretty sure Jonathon's single still too. So there's at least *one* more option. Grant, do you know any guys around town that are available? Ian's wanting to get into the dating pool and—"

"How would I know anyone? I just came back," I snap too quickly.

It's obvious that Trevor's getting under my skin and I hate to show him that. But he's making a point of rubbing it in my face that Ian asked about other people to date. And even though I know it's ridiculous, I wonder how recently he asked about that. If he's still interested. If anything's changed since I started working for him.

But I'm not going to get answers to any of that sitting here right now, and all that's going to happen is my brother is going to keep torturing me until I have some kind of outburst, so it's probably for the best that I just get out now.

"I think I'm going to head up to bed. It's been a long day," I say, sharper than I mean to. Ian gives me a concerned look, but I don't fully meet his eye. I don't want him to see how worked up I am over just the *possibility* that he *might* want to date someone else.

"You sure? I bet the three of us could tackle this problem," Trevor says brightly.

Screw you, I think to myself. I bet people without siblings have way better luck in the romance department without constantly getting sabotaged.

"I'll see you tomorrow," I say to Ian, wishing I had the opportunity to kiss him good night, but Trevor's there to make sure that's impossible. Not that I'm sure I'd even have the guts to do it if he weren't.

"Sweet dreams," he says, smiling. And something about that tone of his is laced with warm suggestion. He's not just being polite. He's trying to plant ideas in my head. He's trying to make me think of *exactly* what kind of dreams I could be having after everything that happened today.

But I'm not complaining. Trevor may be able to cock-block me in real life, but in my dreams, there's nothing to stop me from doing everything I've ever dreamed of with Ian.

"You too," I say with a secret smile of my own before heading inside. I hope going to sleep is going to be as hard for him as it will be for me.

IAN

*T*he next day, after basically rebuilding the picnic table from scratch, it's time for me to coax Grant out into the water again.

"But we just did that yesterday," he protests, whining even as his eyes soak in the sight of me stripping down again.

"Yeah, and the only way you're going to get used to being in the water is to do it every day."

He actually pales. "Every day?"

I chuckle, dropping my shorts. That brings some of the color back to his face. "Come on, it's not so bad, is it?"

He sighs. "I guess not."

"And you've gotta admit you like the view," I tease as I wade back into the water.

"I don't have to admit anything," he says. But he's pulling his shirt off, so I know I won. Once he's stripped down to his boxers, he steps out into the water until he's far enough to grab onto me. He doesn't go for my hand though; he latches onto my shoulder and lets me lead him farther out.

I walk along the bottom of the lake until the water's about up to our waists.

"Doin' okay back there?" I ask.

Grant doesn't answer, so I turn to look at him and he looks just as panicked as ever. He's pale and shaking, his jaw tight and his eyes wide. But slowly, his breathing calms, and then very gingerly, he starts to peel his fingers off of my shoulder.

That's as far as we get that day. Just standing waist-deep in the water without him holding onto me for support. But the next day I coax him even farther, and soon I've got him to the point where he can't touch the bottom and he has to tread water.

By the end of the week, I'm so freaking proud of the progress he's made, but I know I have to push him just a little bit further. I know that he's stronger than he thinks he is and can do more than he expects to be able to.

And I want to see the way he lights up when he realizes he *can* do it.

Even though we've been working closely on the camp and the cabin and I've been giving him daily swimming lessons, there's been nothing else between Grant and me. No more kisses, no more lingering touches or holding hands. There may not have been anything physically happening, but there were plenty of surreptitious looks, bit lips, clenched fists and jaws. There was a lot of willpower being exercised between the two of us, and I know I'm not the only one that feels that tension. That feels the sexual magnetism between us.

I can't be the only one with blue balls.

But it's not just how much I want him physically, because there's something about Grant that just *does it* for me. I can't say what *it* is, but I didn't know it was missing until now. And I don't want to lose it. Grant makes me feel light and free in a way that I never have before, and if I can return that even in some small way by teaching him to swim, then I want to.

"Do you trust me?" I ask him as we're both treading water just past the point where we can touch ground.

He looks at me curiously for a minute, like he's not sure what I'm really asking.

"You know I wouldn't let anything hurt you, right?" I ask, trying to clarify.

He bites his lip in that way that always makes me want to kiss him again, especially out here in the lake where we had our first kiss. He kicks and flails, reaching out to grab my arm for support. I get us back to where we can both stand flat-footed on the bottom of the lake and Grant blows out a quick huff like he's decided something.

"Yeah, I know. I trust you."

I grin. "Get on your back."

Just like I thought they would, his eyes go wide, his mouth dropping open, his shocked expression both adorable and amusing. "What?"

"You heard me," I say, my voice lowering to almost a growl as I move closer to him, right in his personal bubble, our body heat colliding underwater. "Get on your back."

Grant actually shivers, his eyes fluttering closed for just a moment. "I… I don't know how," he says, goosebumps crawling down his arms.

"Just lie back," I say, extending my arm behind him. "I've got you."

"I'm not going to let anything happen to you," I say, pulling my arm around his shoulders. He takes a deep shuddering breath and closes his eyes, letting himself go, leaning back into the water, into my arm.

I bring my other hand up under him and lift him up to the surface of the water.

"Just breathe. You're fine. Let the water cradle your body."

"You know I don't trust it," he says, almost whining.

"But you trust me," I remind him, grinning.

"I never should have admitted that," he groans.

But he's distracted and at this point my hands are just hovering right under him. I'm not touching him, and I'm not sure he realizes he's floating all on his own.

"Okay, I want you to take a deep breath and open your eyes and let it out without moving."

"So bossy," he jokes.

"I know, that's your job, I'm sorry," I tease back. The fact that he's making jokes at all is a good sign that he's not going to have a panic attack and drown us both.

He takes that deep breath, then lets it out, his eyes opening up to the blue skies above, dotted with fluffy white clouds.

"Oh," he says, sounding… disappointed? "Oh!" he realizes he's floating and suddenly starts trying to stay afloat, making himself sink. Luckily, we're in shallow enough water that he can just stand up once he's done freaking out about it.

"Was I just floating?" he asks, already moving toward the shore.

"You were. What'd you think of it?"

"Not my favorite thing, but it is better than drowning, I'll give it that."

I grin. "Not a high bar, but I'll take it."

Once he's on shore, Grant's quick to go for his towel, but I'm almost certain I spot something before he turns around. Something like a tent in his boxers. Not that I blame him. Adrenaline has a way of doing that. But I want to think it's not *just* the adrenaline. I want to think I've got some part in that erection he's trying to hide.

I don't say anything while we're getting dressed, but I've got a little plan. Sort of. Okay, it's more of a rough idea than a plan. But it's something.

"What's left to do in here?" Grant asks, following me into the main cabin. He looks around, admiring our hard work.

It's almost unrecognizable, and most of it's been done since I broke my thumb, so that makes it even more impressive in my opinion.

"Just one thing," I say, grinning at his arched eyebrow. I go to the fridge and pull out two beers. "We've gotta break it in," I say, opening them both—yeah, even with this soft cast thing I can still open a bottle of beer—and handing one to him.

He takes it, looks a little bashful, then smiles, lifting it up. "Cheers."

"Cheers," I say, clinking my bottle to his, taking a long drink. This is about as far as my rough idea got. I'm on my own from here.

"You've got a really nice place here now," Grant says, nodding appreciatively as he looks around. But he's not just looking at the cabin. He's avoiding looking at me. Or at least I think he is. I don't know.

I put my hand on his shoulder and squeeze and immediately his eyes snap to mine.

"Thank you for all of your hard work. I never could have done it without you."

His teeth rake over his bottom lip and he looks down. "There's still a lot of work to do around…"

"There is," I admit. "But there's no one I'd rather have helping me with it," I say, every word completely sincere.

Grant looks up at me like he's trying to decide that himself. His voice is nothing more than a husky whisper when he answers, "I'm happy to be of service."

And then all at once we're kissing. We're kissing like it's the first and the last time, like everything is brand-new but exactly what we're craving. And I can't speak for Grant, but for me, it is. It's everything. Kissing him makes my head spin in the best way. It makes me feel like everything just makes sense. When I'm kissing Grant, I don't have problems.

Well, I have one problem. It's that I'm not inside of him.

My hands start to wander down his body, exploring the lines of him, feeling the warmth of his skin. He doesn't stop me. My fingers get to his belt buckle and his breath catches.

"What are you—?"

"Thanking you for all your help," I say, smiling as I kiss the side of his neck, stroking the front of his shorts. He grunts and bucks his hips into my hand, his length firm and hot in my palm.

I have his shorts on the floor in a matter of seconds and then I'm reaching inside his boxers, my breath coming hard and fast, desperate to touch him after all this time.

"Wait," he pants, pulling back enough to look me in the eye.

"What is it?" I ask, my resolve slipping, hanging on by a frayed thread at this point.

"I... I should thank you too. For the swimming lessons," he says, his fingers skating down my front, sliding along the edge of my belt. My cock's rock hard long before he actually gets to the buckle, but he still seems surprised to find me there, ready to fill his hand, eager to be touched by him.

"Wanna know what's great about this place?" I ask, barely able to make words as he works my shorts down off of me, his fingers closing around me, stroking me, making me dizzy with how damn good it feels.

"What?"

"It's got a bed," I say, forcing myself to pull out of his hand. "Come on."

It's not a long trek to the bedroom, but it's long enough that we're both able to shed what little remaining clothes we have. And once we're next to the bed, I'm on him again in an instant. We're kissing, our limbs tangling together, and before long I turn and I'm kissing down his body, lower and lower, until my lips are right above his hard dick and Grant's got the sheets bunched in his fists in anticipation.

He's panting, breathing so hard, his whole body tense, every muscle coiled tight. And I just hover there. I wait until he actually looks at me, until he's wondering what I'm waiting for.

Then I suck the tip of him. Just enough to make his whole body go rigid, a soft gasp ripping from his lips. I stroke him in my hand and focus my mouth on the crown of his cock, driving him wild, but never giving him enough, never going quite far enough to push him over that edge.

"Ian," he pants. "Ian, please. Oh God, *fuck*, please," he mutters, thrashing on the bed as I slowly lower my lips, letting my tongue swirl around him lazily.

Then I suck in a sharp breath, *my* whole body going still as his warm, wet mouth slips over the head of *my* cock. I groan as his lips sink further and further, taking in my whole length. Grant groans too and the vibrations go straight through my cock to my balls, making them tighten up. Fuck, he feels so good. *This* feels so good.

It's one thing to have him making me feel good, but it's the hottest fucking thing in the world to listen to the sounds he makes as I suck him off. The little grunting gasping mewls are addicting and I'm learning just how to swirl my tongue, just how to move my lips to make them happen.

Grant's hand cups my balls, stroking them as his mouth works its magic, making my eyes roll back in my head, my blood boil with the need to come. It was bad enough when I was just thinking about Grant and fantasizing about him, but now, having him in my bed, actually touching him, tasting him, hearing him…

Fuck, it's almost too much to bear.

I roar and pull back from him. It's too good, it's too much. "Fuck, Grant, I'm gonna—oh *shit*." He hollows his cheeks as I try to warn him and he sucks even harder, his lips milking me, making it impossible to hold back as the orgasm crashes through me like a freight train, my vision going blurry as I shoot rope after rope of sticky salty cum down his throat.

He didn't even try to get out of swallowing, I think as my body convulses once more.

Even while I'm still trembling with the aftershocks of what Grant just did to me, I'm very aware that he still hasn't come. I wrap my lips around him again, sucking him base to tip, base to tip, until he's panting and I pull off of him, trailing suckling nibbles down his shaft, over his balls, and then I stick my tongue in his ass.

Grant jolts off the bed, his back arching, a cry echoing from the rafters.

"Ian... Oh... Oh God," he gasps as my tongue swirls around his puckered opening, darting in and out, fucking his ass with my tongue as I reach up and stroke him.

"No one's ever... I never..."

I grin. "You've never had anyone eat your ass?" Just for punctuation, I slide my tongue deep inside him again and he bucks up like he's been touched with a live wire.

"N-n-no," he pants.

"You like my tongue in your ass," I say. It's not a question. There's no doubt he's fucking loving this.

"Y-y-y-oh *God*, yes."

"You're going to come for me with my tongue in your ass. You're going to come all over my hand while I fuck your ass with my mouth."

He *moans* like I've never heard and then his whole body seizes.

"Ian!" he cries, and it's the best thing I've ever heard. A second later, his hot sticky semen is all over my hand and my wrist. I suck him clean before I crawl up his body, kissing him, letting him taste himself, tasting myself, tasting the mixture of us. That alone is enough to make my dick twitch again.

But instead of trying anything else, I just pull Grant close to me and kiss the side of his head, so damn happy to just have him here.

"Ian?" he asks after a few minutes of lying in the still and the quiet of this secluded cabin.

"Yeah?"

"What's happening between us?"

I sigh. I was afraid he'd have questions like this. Afraid because I don't really have an answer for him.

"I don't know," I admit. "But it feels right."

He nods, abusing that bottom lip again.

"What?"

"Trevor will object," he says.

"I know." I sigh, holding him a little tighter. "Believe me, I know. And I don't want to lose my best friend after losing so much else recently, but I don't want to give this up either. I don't want to lose you." I'm not sure where this is all coming from, but I know it's true. I know losing Grant sounds like one of the worst things that could happen to me right now.

"Maybe we should take a break… Try to figure out—"

"No," I say, stopping him before he can talk himself out of this. "I don't want a break when we're only just starting. Why don't we go camping this weekend? Maybe kayaking? Just us. We'll see how things go without having to worry about what anyone else sees or thinks."

Grant stiffens and pulls back from me, frowning. "I'm not going to be your dirty little secret, Ian."

"I don't want you to be," I say immediately. "I'd never expect you to be. I've had enough secrets and living in the shadows, you know that."

He sighs and snuggles back into me. "Yeah, I do. Okay, why not. I haven't been kayak camping since Boy Scouts."

"I'm surprised you've been at all with your aversion to water."

He makes a face and it's so damn cute I have to kiss the tip of his nose. "I had to do it for a badge, but at least in kayaking you get a flotation device by default. If you use one in swimming, everyone makes fun of you."

"I wouldn't make fun of you."

He gives me a look.

"But you've been before? You know what you're doing?"

He laughs and nods. "Enough. I know camping. Kayaking is iffier, but how hard can it be? Do you have a kayak?"

"No, but Trevor told me that Garrett's got some kind of outdoor adventure company now?" At this point, I don't think there's a business in town that's not run by a Rainier or someone related to them.

"Oh yeah… Well, you know my parents have a bunch of stuff too."

I make a face. "Do they have a double kayak? And if they do, do you want them to know that's what we're taking?" He eyes my hand, and I smile again. "Even with the broken thumb excuse."

He sighs, then shakes his head. "No, you're probably right. You should rent from Garrett. I don't think he's got anyone to tell anyway."

"So that's a yes to the camping trip?

He smirks, but I've worn him down, there's no doubt. "Yes."

"It'll be fun," I say, kissing him.

He smiles. "Says the guy that's going to pawn all the paddling off to me because of his broken thumb."

"Maybe I'll make it up to you in other ways," I tease, pressing my hips forward.

His cheeks turn pink and he tries to hide in the covers but I won't let him.

"I could maybe live with that," he admits in a whisper.

Then he sighs and pulls away from me. "I should get home before anyone wonders where I am and comes looking."

I frown, but know he's right. Never underestimate the Rainiers or their desire to protect their own.

"Tomorrow morning then? Thistle River?"

He nods. "I'll see you then."

I linger around behind him as he gets dressed and follow him to the door, stealing one last kiss before he leaves. Maybe it's too much. Maybe it's overboard, but it feels right. And with Grant, I'm just following my gut. I don't know what I'm doing or what to expect, but I know that when I'm with him, nothing else matters and I want to keep experiencing that for as long as I possibly can.

GRANT

*I*t's early. Super early. So early that the sun's not even really up yet. The sky is just kind of a hazy gray-blue and there's still mist clinging to the ground. I'm hoping that if I get out of here early enough, no one will notice and ask me where I'm going.

Pre-dawn seems early enough.

I love the smell this time of morning; that clean pure scent of dew on grass, the faintest lingering sweetness from the spring flowers.

I've got my bags packed and loaded already. All that's left is to get the kayak strapped to the car. Ian texted to let me know that Garrett didn't have any double-kayaks in stock this weekend on short notice, so I wanted to get out of here before anyone's around to ask questions about where I'm going and who I'm going with, taking this one.

As soon as I've got it in the air, I remember where I'm going and who I'm going with and I nearly drop it.

I still can't believe I agreed to a camping weekend with Ian.

I'm so excited.

I'm so nervous.

But also excited.

But I also think I might be completely insane for thinking this has a snowball's chance in hell of going well. Maybe Ian's just rubbing off on me and I'm getting more willing to take risks. I mean really. *Kayaking?!* What was I thinking? I'm not the kind of guy who goes kayaking. I'm the kind of guy that panics at the sight of a puddle because it could drown him.

Although that's not really as true as it used to be, I realize. Not since my swimming lessons with Ian.

Besides, it's not like I could ever say no to him. He wanted a weekend away with me. He could ask me to hide in a bunker with him and I'd say yes in a heartbeat.

I know it's terrible to be so smitten with my brother's best friend, and I know Trevor'd have a fit if he found out, but what he doesn't know won't hurt him, right?

The sun creeps higher above the horizon, giving me enough light to finish securing one of the family's kayaks to my car. It's not like I have my own, but my family has every outdoor sport accessory a person could want. One of the few benefits of living so far away from civilization *and* owning one of the only eateries in town. There's a reason the second garage was built to house stuff other than cars.

The birds are happy to see the sun, greeting it with their merry songs and I feel like I'm in a movie scene or something. Everything's going right, it's a beautiful morning, I have a date with the guy I've been crushing on for the last decade or more, birds are singing… It's just perfect.

But it's not just birds singing I hear. There's footsteps pounding up the dirt drive. Heavy breathing. Someone running. I run through about a dozen scenarios of lost hikers or bear attack victims showing up on our property before Trevor comes around the corner and jogs right over to me, squinting in the early morning light.

"What are you doing up so early?" he asks.

"Could ask you the same."

He's breathing heavily, sweating, and pulls out a water bottle, chugging it down.

"Running," he says, like it should be obvious.

I mean, it should be. But I wasn't expecting to see him right now and I really *don't* want to see him right now.

"I didn't know you ran…"

He shrugs. "What're you up to?"

I freeze, complete and total panic gripping me. I look up over my shoulder to the kayak strapped to the roof of my car, and I know he sees it. He has to see it. It's a freaking kayak strapped to a car. So it's not like I can just pretend it's not there. I have to think of something that sounds plausible involving the kayak.

"I'm uh… going… kayak… camping."

Damn it, Grant. That's not even a lie.

Trevor's eyebrows go really high and he looks at the kayak again like he thinks it's a trick or something.

"Are you really?"

"Mm-hmm," I say, wincing, knowing how dumb it sounds even though it's the truth. I really don't have a better answer for him and I wish I did.

"Shit, I'll join in on that action. Sounds fun. Do you mind?"

"Um… actually…" I search and search for some reason to say no, to deny him, but he looks so damn hopeful and if he ever found out the truth after I told him he couldn't come… Yeah, I didn't want to deal with that possible fallout.

"Yeah, the more the merrier," I say, mentally punching myself the whole time. Ian is going to hate me. *I* hate me. This was supposed to be some kind of chance to see what could happen between us. To see where this thing might go. And now my big brother's going to tag along.

Fuck.

"Who else is going?"

Why did I ever have to open my big, dumb mouth?

"Just… just Ian," I say. I can't even lie about this. I could have said anything. I could have made someone up and then made up an excuse about why he couldn't make it at the last minute. But no. I default to truth and that is literally the worst possible answer.

I know it's the worst possible answer because Trevor's eyes narrow and get hard and I think for a minute he might actually yell at me or even punch me. If the stories are to be believed, he and Sawyer used to get into fist fights and wrestling matches all the time, but Mom would never let them roughhouse with me, so I got all the pranks. Not sure which I'd prefer, but right now I'm really hoping I'm not going to get an introduction to the physical abuse side to having siblings.

But he doesn't punch me and he doesn't yell. He lets out a slow breath and rolls his shoulders back.

"Where are you guys meeting?"

"Thistle River."

"I'll meet you there in an hour."

I nod and he just turns and jogs up to the house. I feel like I've just dodged a bullet, but in doing so I've stepped right in the line of a firing squad.

It's not a good feeling.

Regardless, I wipe the sweat off my palms and head off to meet Ian. And break the good news to him.

"He what?"

"He just sort of… invited himself along."

Ian growls and slams his hand into his truck, then jumps

back with a curse, shaking it because it's his injured hand and he's being a dumb caveman.

"I'm sorry." I know he's disappointed. I am too. This was supposed to be…

Well, it doesn't matter what it was supposed to be, because that's not what it's going to be.

"Don't be. It's not your fault. I know how he is. It's just… annoying."

When he says that, his voice gets lower. He moves closer to me and his hand lands on my hip. He pulls me to him.

"It is really annoying," I agree.

"I guess we're just going to have to make the best out of an unfortunate situation," he says.

I blink, then lean into him a little more. "You mean you still want to do it?"

"Of course I do. I'm serious about this. About you… about figuring out what it could be. Even if your brother insists on getting in my way."

"Oh yeah?" I grin, leaning up to kiss him but jerking away before I can because I hear tires on gravel and I know it's probably Trevor.

Sure enough, it's the walking cockblock himself.

"Barrett," he says, nodding his head as he gets out of his truck.

"Rainier," Ian says back, helping him unload his stuff.

"Don't do that, it's going to get confusing," I say, already regretting having them both here. This is going to be a nightmare.

"Figured he'd have some other name for you with all the time you two have been spending alone together," Trevor says, the comment clearly aimed at Ian.

"Watch it," Ian says, stepping up. "He's working for me. How do you expect us to not spend time together?"

"That's not—"

"Could you not?" I butt in. "We haven't even loaded up the kayaks yet and you guys are making me regret even agreeing to go on this trip. So if this is how it's going to be, let me know and I'll just go back home now."

Trevor looks like he's going to say something else, but then he sees Ian's face, and Ian's glaring at him like I've never witnessed. Apparently Trevor hasn't either because it works and he doesn't say anything.

"Sorry," he says instead.

"Me too," Ian says.

"Let's try to have fun, huh?" Trevor says, unusually peppy for him. Ian notices it too and gives me a look, but we both seem independently to decide not to say anything about it.

"Sounds like a plan," I say, trying my best not to sound sarcastic about it. I don't exactly have high hopes for this weekend, but at least I don't expect any of us to die, so I guess it could be worse?

We load up the kayaks and head out down to the river. Ian and Trevor apparently used to camp this trail a lot when they were growing up, so as usual, I'm just following their lead.

But this time is different. Because Trevor doesn't have all of Ian's attention. In fact, Ian's practically ignoring him—not on purpose, I don't think—and it seems to actually be getting to my dear older brother. Who knew?

When we reach the shore, Trevor doesn't hesitate, throwing his life jacket on like it's nothing, while I take my time, trying to fasten the straps of my own with trembling hands. Then I feel Ian's hand on my back, and he gives me a look of such confidence that I know everything is still going to be okay. Ian's got my back.

And all the rest of me.

~

"Lunch?" Ian calls.

Automatically, my stomach grumbles, not that anyone else hears it. I still glare at it. No need to be so dramatic.

"Sounds good to me," I answer.

"Sure," says Trevor.

They scout for a good place to pull ashore and we make sure the boats are tied up before unpacking anything.

"I brought you sandwiches," I tell Ian. He grins and then we both look guiltily at Trevor. "I… didn't pack for you," I say apologetically.

"It's fine," he says, pulling a bag of jerky out of his pack. Ian gives me another look and I groan.

"Are you sure you don't want half of mine?" I offer.

"Grant, it's fine. If I wanted a sandwich, I would have made one and packed it myself. Thanks, but I don't want it."

"Got it," I mutter, shaking my head to the concerned look Ian sends me. If there's anyone that understands what an ass my brother can be, it's Ian. But, whatever. I'm used to it.

We sit around on some nearby fallen logs that campers before us have arranged in a convenient seating arc, eating in silence, the sounds of nature deafening because no one's saying anything.

It's just made worse by the fact that I'm sitting next to Ian and everything in me just wants to lean into him, but Trevor's right there and I know it would be a whole thing.

But Ian doesn't reach out for me either, and it makes me self-conscious. I keep thinking about him saying he wants to figure out what this could be, but then I see how he acts when Trevor's around and I'm not so sure. Actions speak louder than words, and it seems like he'd rather end things than admit to Trevor that we're…

Whatever the hell we are.

Dating hardly seems right, since we haven't really been on a date. This *could* have been one. Thanks a lot, Trevor.

Friends with benefits, maybe? What happened yesterday definitely seems like it should be classified as a benefit. But I don't know. I don't know what Ian's thinking and that drives me crazy.

I know one thing. I don't want to be anyone's hook-up. Especially not Ian's. My feelings for Ian are…

Well, they're complicated, but I know they're too much for me to just be a meaningless fling to him. I really like Ian. And I think it could possibly, maybe, be more than *like* with some nurturing and encouragement, but that's only going to happen if we both want it to, and I just don't know.

But as the day goes on, we all start to relax a bit. It probably doesn't hurt that there's beer in Ian's cooler. By the time we hit land again to make camp for the night, we're all laughing and having a good time and the tension from earlier in the day is gone.

Trevor goes off to gather wood while Ian sets up the tents and I'm relegated to trying to start a fire.

It's not easy. All that mist and dew from this morning must have been the remnants of a storm that hit farther downstream because everything around here is still soaked and I can't get anything to catch.

"What's wrong, Boy Scout?" Ian teases, hearing me curse at the fire for probably the hundredth time.

"Shut up. I only take flak from people with two operable thumbs."

"Touché."

Trevor comes tromping back in and drops a sad pile of twigs down near me.

"Really?" I ask, incredulous.

"Everything's soaked."

"No kidding," I say, gesturing to the lack of fire.

"Do you want me to try?" Ian asks.

"I'll just be annoyed if you get it going at this point," I say, completely determined. I get the driest kindling I can find and place a little wad of cotton on top. I light it and let it spark, breathing on it gently, watching the ember glow.

"Any luck?"

I hold up a hand to Trevor, but even that makes my tiny flame dance wildly.

Slowly, I lower it down to the brush pile on the ground. This is where it goes wrong every time. This stuff is too damp for the ember to catch.

But somehow, maybe with the power of all of our wills collectively focused on it, the ember catches and crackles to life, the tiniest wisp of smoke curling up into the air.

"Way to go, Boy Scout!" Ian cheers, the tents all but set up at this point.

"Knew you could do it," Trevor says, clapping me on the shoulder. It's probably the most complimentary thing he's ever said to me.

"What's for dinner?" I ask Ian. "You are cooking, right?"

"You're lucky I am," he teases. He opens up his cooler and pulls out a carefully-wrapped foil packet. "Skewers and rice," he says. "Any objections?"

"Beats what I've got," Trevor says.

"I've been waiting for you to cook for me," I say, grinning at him.

He looks a little confused, but he's smiling anyway. "Have you?"

"Well… Yeah. I've only brought you like a dozen lunches by now. You kind of owe me."

His smile just grows. "Guess I do."

"Let's get those babies on the fire," Trevor says.

I realize we were flirting openly in front of him, and regardless of anything else, that's not very sensitive when I know Trevor's uncomfortable. Yes, he's going to have to get over it eventually, but I can't expect that to magically happen at the snap of my fingers. I hope he's trying to keep an open mind today, that he's trying to be in a good mood despite the... implications of this trip. So I don't really want to make it any harder than it needs to be. We're all adults and we can act like it.

The skewers are really good.

"What kind of marinade did you use on those?" Trevor asks, licking his fingers.

Ian shrugs. "Just something I threw together. Little of this, little of that."

"It was really, really good," I say, also licking my fingers, but probably not for the same reason. I'm doing it because I keep catching Ian looking at me while I do. I'm doing it because I like the hungry look in his eyes. I like how I can glance down at his lap and see how I'm affecting him.

Yeah, it's not really fair to tease him like this, but it's *fun*, and I know if he had his chance he'd do the same damn thing. So I'm taking the opportunity while I've got it.

"You eventually get sick of having take-out every night," Ian says, looking up, " and you start to miss a home-cooked meal. Too bad I couldn't have gotten your mom to deliver to me."

"You should be glad you never asked her to. She might have. Besides, her meat's never that satisfying." The last thing I add under my breath, low enough that only he can hear it.

Ian's in the middle of drinking his beer and I swear it comes out of his nose as soon as I say it. Trevor frowns across the fire at us.

"What was that?"

"Nothing..." I say innocently.

He lifts his brows and I roll my eyes, sighing. I already planned for this. I knew he'd butt in. That's okay.

I look critically at my skewer. "Not everyone's got the hang of handling sticks of meat."

Trevor snorts his beer too and I swear I see Ian give me an appreciative look out of the corner of my eye.

"Well, I slept like shit last night and I know we've got another day ahead of us tomorrow, so I'm gonna hit the hay," Trevor says, standing, stretching, yawning. He looks at the two of us, his face stern and hard, and he looks like he has something to say, but whatever it is, he decides not to say it, instead ducking into one of the tents with his sleeping bag.

"Fire's getting low," Ian says, nudging the embers with a long stick. He breaks it into pieces and tosses it on the pile.

"Yeah, I was thinking about looking for some wood."

He grins. "I'll come with you. Maybe I can help you find it."

There's no mistaking the heat in his tone, and I shiver at the look he's giving me.

We wanted to see how things developed. This certainly seems like a development.

But I need to play it cool. Maybe he's legitimately just talking about firewood. Maybe I'm getting ahead of myself and getting my hopes up for nothing.

I get up slowly and grab my flashlight before heading off into the trees away from camp, the sound of Ian's steady footfalls close behind. Soon we're far enough away that I can't even see the glow of the fire anymore. It's so dark I can hardly see anything, just the barest of shadows in the sliver of moonlight. But I see Ian. I see him moving toward me, a dark shape in the night, and he's coming at me fast.

He pins me against a tree, the bark scraping against my back, like his lips are rough against mine. He's demanding and possessive, his tongue plunging into my mouth without asking permission, without waiting for me to be ready for it.

I cling to him, holding onto his shirt, gasping for breath, desperate for more.

"You've been driving me fucking crazy all day," he growls,

biting my neck hard enough to make me gasp, but the jolt of pain feels so *good*. It feels so right.

"I don't know what you're talking about," I say innocently, even though there's nothing innocent about the way I sound, my voice all breathy moans and hitched cries as he grinds his hips into mine.

"I think you do," he says, grabbing my wrist to pull my hand up to his lips, sucking one of my fingers *deep* in his mouth. I drop my head back and groan, my dick surging in my pants, my blood on fire with need for this man. This man I never expected to have a chance with that's currently sucking on my fingers in the middle of the woods.

Crazy, I know.

He slowly pulls his lips back from my finger until it leaves his mouth with a *pop.* He doesn't let go of my wrist; instead he holds it above my head and kisses me again. He kisses me like it's the last time he might ever do it. Like he's wanted nothing more for so long and I can feel every bit of that as his teeth drag over my bottom lip and he groans into me.

"Take your pants off," he says. "Take your pants off and turn around."

I'm already obeying him, my pants around my knees when the realization hits me.

"Ian… I haven't… I mean… You're the only—"

He drags me against him and kisses me senseless again. "Do you want this?"

"More than anything," I answer without thinking.

"You still trust me?" he asks.

I nod, but then realize it's still too dark to really see. My eyes are adjusting, but even then, there's only so much light way out here.

"Yes. I do. And I want you so fucking much."

"Good, now turn around."

I obey him without a thought. I don't know what it is, but

Ian just brings out this part of me that wants to obey him. He's so in charge and dominant when it comes to sex and I'm so inexperienced, that it seems like a perfect match.

"Hug the tree and don't you dare let go."

The tree I'm up against is young enough that I can just get my arms around it and link my fingers. That's a really good thing, because I need the support when Ian slides his hands down the back of my legs, dragging my pants down to my ankles. He nudges my feet back and as far apart as they'll go, so I'm just standing in the middle of the woods, half-naked, hugging a tree with my ass exposed to the whole world.

And I've never been more turned on in my entire life.

His hands run back up the insides of my legs and then he's touching my ass, spreading my cheeks. I expect to feel his finger or his cock, but I nearly jump out of my skin when it's his tongue licking me, diving into my deepest parts.

"Ian... God, that feels so good."

"I love the way you squirm when my tongue's in your ass. It makes me want to bury my cock inside of it and see what you do then."

I turn to look at him over my shoulder, never letting go of the tree. My cock's so hard that I'm leaking precum and my balls are tight enough that they're actually painful, but it's such a good pain that I don't even mind.

I want more.

So, so much more.

"You should do it then," I say, trying to taunt him.

"Oh, should I?" His tongue curls against me and I grunt into the tree bark, trying not to scream loud enough to wake up Trevor.

"Mm-hmm. Yes. Yes, you should."

"Sounds like you've thought about this," he says, standing up behind me, kissing the back of my neck as I hear his zipper come undone.

"Have you been thinking about my hard cock inside of you, Grant?"

I whimper as he rubs the head of his dick along the cleft of my ass.

"Well?"

"*Yes*," I groan, anticipation alone nearly enough to make me come right then and there.

"You're lucky I came prepared for just such an occasion," he says. There's a snap, like a lid opening, and some kind of squelching and the next thing I know his fingers are at my hole and they're covered in what I realize must be lube.

"Thinking you might get lucky, huh?" I say, trying to be coy even as he slides a finger in my ass and my eyes roll back in my head.

"Between you and me, it kind of seemed like a sure thing." He slides another finger inside of me and I'm shaking, my legs trembling with the effort of holding me up.

"Ian…" My voice is shaking as much as my knees and he brings me *so* close. So close that I'm *sure* there's no way I'm *not* coming. But then he pulls back, his fingers leaving me empty and wanting, and leans forward to press his lips against my ear.

"Tell me what you want."

I whine and try to just arch my ass back toward him, but there's only so far I can go without letting go of the tree. I feel like if I do that, this spell, whatever's happening right now, will be over.

"You can do it. Tell me how much you want me to fuck you and it'll be all yours."

I hear a condom wrapper rip open and then, as if to emphasize his point, Ian presses the tip of his lube-covered cock against my opening. He just rocks forward ever so slightly, stretching me just enough to make me know what I'm missing.

I hate that he's making me say this out loud, but I also love it. I love how dirty he makes me. How desired it makes me feel. It's addicting.

"Ian," I pant, trying again to move my hips back, but this time it's just for show, just to get that growl from deep inside his chest, while he slides the condom on. "Ian, I want you to fuck me. Please fuck me… Fill my tight ass until I scream."

"God*damn*," he growls, pushing into me with a slow, steady stroke. I want more. I want it hard and fast and merciless, but I know he's trying to be gentle because it's my first time like this. I know he's taking care of me, the way he said he would.

And I'll be damned if that doesn't make the whole thing sexier somehow. Because I know there will be time for fucking raw and hard until neither of us knows which way is up, but there will never be another first time with Ian. This slow, measured entry is everything I want and more.

And then, all at once, he's fully inside of me. He's filling me so perfectly, and I'm stretched so tight around him that it's hard to tell where he stops and I start. We're one being, lost in lust and passion and pleasure. So much pleasure.

"You feel perfect," he says, his voice sending shivers down my spine.

"You too," I pant back, my body alive with electricity, every nerve sparking with the sensations his cock is sending through me.

He pumps in and out of me, slow at first, then harder, faster, until I can't breathe, I can't think. It's so good that I forget everything I know. Everything except one thing. All I know is I want him. *All* of him.

"I want you to come inside of me," I say, the words surprising even me. Ian grunts and pulls back, pumping into me forcefully, making me cry out, clutching the tree, my whole body overwhelmed with Ian. He's inside me, around me, consuming me. And I love it. I love it so much. It's not like anything I could have imagined. It's so much better, so much realer. It's desperate and needy and my veins are pulsing with pure pleasure as he rams into me.

"You're going to come with my big cock inside of you, aren't you, Grant?"

"Oh God, yes!" I cry, my nails digging into the tree bark. "Ian, you're going to make me come so hard... Oh God..."

There's no stopping it once it starts and Ian just keeps hammering away, driving me higher and higher until I think my body might actually overload from how good it all feels. He holds me tight, his fingers digging into my sides as he bites my shoulder. I feel him swell inside of me and it's the most amazing thing I've ever felt. I feel so full and so sexy and I feel him jerking and convulsing inside my body. I feel *claimed*. It's so raw and unbridled. It's deep and real and there's some connection between us that's more than just his cock buried in me, making us both dizzy with pleasure.

I feel like this might actually be going somewhere. Somewhere deeper than sex. And I hope that's not just me being naive. But at least for this one moment, I'm going to enjoy being with him and feeling all those things and not worry about it or try to come up with all the ways it can go wrong. I think I deserve that much.

IAN

*G*rant's hand is in mine as we walk back to the camp and I keep bringing it up to my lips, kissing the back of his knuckles. All I want is to hold him close, to stare into his eyes and run my fingers through his hair.

Yeah, I'm feeling sappy and tender and I don't know why, but there it is.

Okay, so I might know why. I might have an idea of what's going on. But it's a terrifying thought. Or at least I know it should be. With Grant, it's hard for me to be scared of falling for him.

And I am. There's no denying it. Even before sex was a thing between us, I've been feeling things for him. Things I know I shouldn't, but can't deny no matter how hard I try.

There's something special about this guy. Something that makes me think he might just be the one for me. And I'm definitely worried that I'm getting ahead of myself, but there are no brakes on this train. He makes me think crazy things about settling down, committing, making a life together.

Things I've never thought about before. Of course, I was never out before either. Being free to live my life openly presents a whole lot of new doors, but it's also uncharted territory.

Grant's walking close to me in the dark as we near camp, and as I see the glow of the fire grow closer, I stop and squeeze his hand.

"We actually should grab some wood."

He doesn't say anything, but his flashlight comes on and we spend a few minutes looking around, finding a couple of sticks and some dry brush. It's not much, but it's enough to cover our tracks and keep the fire alive through most of the night.

At least with our arms full of fuel for the fire, we're not holding hands anymore, but when we come back to camp together and Trevor's awake, sitting by the fire, I know that he knows. Plausible deniability or not, he knows.

"What the hell," he says, his voice tight in that quiet angry tone that's always so much worse than just yelling. "The minute I look the other way you two are sneaking around behind my back?"

"We were just…" Grant says, holding up his sticks, tossing some on the fire. "For the fire…"

"Bullshit. I'm not an idiot. I know when I'm being lied to. I *trusted* you," he says, glaring daggers at me. Grant recoils, almost moving to hide behind me to shield himself from the anger radiating off of Trevor in palpable waves.

But I've had enough. I'm not going to be intimidated into not dating someone I want to date. Period.

"I like your brother, so what?" I snap, hot anger boiling up inside me too fast to put a lid on it.

"So what? I told you to stay away from him!"

"Well too bad. I'm not going to. We're dating and you're just going to have to get over it. No matter how much you complain, your *adult* brother can make his own decisions and

I'm not going to stop seeing him just because it makes you uncomfortable."

Trevor looks like I might as well have just punched him, his face twisting up even angrier, dark and menacing. But we've been friends for years. We've been in our fair share of fights. If we have to duke this out all the way, so be it. Bring it on.

I'm not afraid to fight for Grant.

"I know how you are and I don't want my little brother to be just another one of your random flings that gets tossed aside and heartbroken. You want him now, but when you shatter him, who's going to have to pick up the pieces?"

Some of the anger leaves me. I remind myself that Trevor's just being protective. He's looking out for his youngest sibling. And I can't blame him. I can't even argue with his accusations.

"Does he know?" Trevor presses. "Does he know what a manwhore you are? Different guy every day of the week, none of them lasting more than a night or two. Or did you conveniently leave that part out while you were trying to take advantage of him?"

"He's not—" Grant says, but I turn and the look I give him stops his words in his tracks.

"He's not wrong, Grant," I say. "That's how I've always been. I've always had a string of short, discreet, *meaningless* flings to hide my sexuality during my career. And to be honest, if I were still playing baseball and hadn't been outed to my team, this whole situation might be a lot different. I'd probably still just be looking for sex. But I'm not. Things are different now. I'm free to live my life the way I choose and I want more than that. I want something real. And I've already told you I'm in the market for a good man," I say, flashing him a grin.

Grant looks concerned about this new development, but after chewing on his lip for a few moments, he nods.

"I believe you," he says.

Having Grant on my side, knowing that he trusts me, releases a knot of tension in my chest that I didn't even realize was there. Feeling a bit freer, lighter, I turn back to my best friend.

"Look, I understand that you're just looking out for Grant and trying to keep in mind what's best for him, but he's a big boy now and can make his own decisions. And you should know me, man. I'm not going to hurt Grant if there's anything I can do to help it. He's not just some fling. If that's all this was, there's no way I'd jeopardize our friendship over it."

Trevor's still glaring at me, but he looks past me to Grant. I don't know what he sees in his brother, but it's something that seems to change the tide in my favor a little.

"I swear, if you hurt him—"

"I know," I say, nodding. "I'll help you kick my ass."

He grumbles under his breath, but he's clearly not interested in arguing with us anymore.

"Fine, but don't say I didn't warn you." He still sounds pissed, but at least there's not going to be any more fighting tonight because he's heading back into his tent.

I turn to Grant and he lets out a long shaky breath.

"I didn't expect that to go so well," he says.

I grin. "That was well?"

He shrugs, giving me a sheepish smile. "It's not like he's ever met anyone I dated before... You're getting the first boyfriend treatment."

"I like the sound of that," I say, wrapping my arm around his waist, pulling him in for a kiss.

"You know, my sleeping bag's big enough for two," I whisper in his ear.

He arches a brow. "You really *did* come prepared to get lucky, didn't you?"

I grin. "Can't blame a guy for being hopeful, can you?"

He shakes his head, but he's grinning too and I know he's flattered by it if nothing else.

I head over to the other tent, my sleeping bag already set up inside, and start stripping down to my boxers, knowing Grant's eyes are on me without even looking to confirm.

It's not just his eyes that are on me. He surprises me, his hands molding to my skin from behind, tracing the lines of my shoulders, skimming down my spine. I shiver, and pull him into me.

"Come to bed," I rumble.

He doesn't take his eyes off of mine as he undresses, leaving his clothes in a neat pile next to mine. And then we both crawl into the tent. It's a little awkward trying to get us both in the sleeping bag, but once we manage, it's nice and cozy. I've got my arms around him, his head's on my chest, and I'm just listening to the mingling of our heartbeats mixing with the sounds of the forest at night.

"I knew, you know. That you were kind of a player," he says.

My chest tightens and I feel guilty. It somehow seems like a betrayal to Grant that I've been with so many other people. And now I know why they were so unsatisfying. I know why they were never enough.

Because they weren't him.

They didn't have this connection, this spark that drives me wild and makes me forget which way is up.

"I'm sorry," I say, not knowing what else *to* say. There's nothing I can do about the past, but I can try to be better going forward.

"Why?" he asks, turning to me, his face confused.

I shrug. "I don't know. It just seems... unfair that I've been with so many people and you... haven't."

"But out of all those people, you're happy with me?"

I kiss his forehead and tighten my arms around him. "I am."

"See, that makes it even better."

"Oh, so I shouldn't get too cocky about you liking me since you just don't know any better?" I tease, the sound of Trevor's beer-induced snores rumbling through the tent. At least I don't have to worry about him eavesdropping on our conversation.

Grant chuckles at me and shakes his head. "That could be the case but... It's not. Don't worry."

"Oh?" Now he's got my curiosity piqued.

"Oh God, never mind. I shouldn't have said anything," he groans, burying his face in my chest.

I run my hand down his back, grinning. "Oh, but you did. And now you have to spill."

"Ugh... You're so mean," he whines, but even as he does, he moves his body against me and I feel the firmness between his legs. I know how much me teasing him and making him admit things turns him on.

"Well?"

"I've... I've kind of had a crush on you for... ever, basically. So, I guess you could *say* I don't know any better, but the truth is that I've never really wanted anything else. When I was at college... I fooled around a little, but nothing ever serious. Nothing like this. Nothing like what I always wanted... with you."

"And? Does reality match up to the fantasy, or is it woefully disappointing?"

He laughs and the warm sound washes through my body, heating my blood, making me want him all over again. There's no denying it. This man drives me crazy in the best possible ways. But I don't know how I'm ever going to stop thinking with my dick when I'm around him. It's like he shuts off the switch to my brain and there's only one head I can use.

"No," he answers, his voice soft and dreamy. "Definitely not disappointing."

I smile and hold him close, nothing at all wrong in this moment. With Grant in my arms, everything's perfect.

It takes a little while longer and we still talk off and on, but eventually the sounds of Trevor's snores lull us to sleep.

GRANT

*I*t's been about a week since the kayak camping trip and Ian and I have been pretty much inseparable since then. Trevor's still annoyed but he's getting over it, and Scout teases me pretty much every morning, but I can tell she's just happy for me. I haven't exactly told the parents, because you never tell your parents about someone brand-new, but telling them about *Ian* this soon seems extra naive. So my siblings are the only ones that know for now, and that's plenty, believe me.

I'm trying not to think too much about how my siblings are reacting to the whole thing, because that just puts extra unnecessary pressure on the delicate beginning stages of the relationship. But I know I'm happy with Ian and I want to see where this keeps going.

We're working on rebuilding the lifeguard tower—his thumb's almost totally better by now and he should be able to take the cast off next week—when I get a phone call. I finish securing the board that Ian's holding up and then we both step back and I answer the phone.

I haven't mentioned it to my family, but Ian knows that

I've already started putting out job applications. There's no point in waiting if I want to move to the city in a month or so. I haven't heard anything back from anyone, but these things take time.

Still, I'm kind of surprised to see the area code from the city, and when I answer, my voice is a little shaky.

"Hello?"

"Yes, I'm calling for Mr. Grant Rainier?"

"Speaking."

"I'm calling from the Lyrett County Office of Urban Planning and Development. We received your resume in response to a job opening we posted."

"Yes?" I'm pacing and Ian's looking at me like I've lost my mind, but my heart's beating a thousand miles a minute and I think I might be having a heart attack or something and she hasn't even told me anything yet.

"We were wondering if you'd be willing to come in for an interview this week?"

"Yes! Of course," I say too quickly. "I'd love to. When's a convenient time for you?"

"We're conducting our interviews Wednesday through Friday, ten a.m. to three p.m. Do you have a preference?"

"I'll take the first slot available," I tell her. There's no way I'm going to sit back while someone else goes in a day earlier and makes a great impression and gets the job I want. No thanks.

"Okay, that will be Wednesday at twelve thirty. We'll see you then."

"Sounds great, thank you so much."

As I hang up the phone, Ian's giving me a questioning look and I'm still shaking, but I manage to grin at him.

"I've got an interview," I say, still kind of in disbelief about the whole thing.

His eyes go wide and he's on me in a second, wrapping me up in his arms and kissing me. It's the best celebration.

"Congratulations."

"Thanks," I say, still smiling, but now reality's settling in and I'm remembering all the things that come with an interview. Finding the right suit, preparing for the questions, making sure I'm there on time and don't get lost trying to navigate the maze of one-way streets downtown looking for a parking garage.

"What's wrong?" Ian asks, picking up on it without me saying anything at all.

"Just suddenly realizing how much I have to do to get ready for it."

"Would it help if you had moral support? I can drive you…"

"Really?" I don't even have to think about his offer for it to start to make me feel better. I'm much more relaxed when Ian's around, and I know having him there to give me a pep talk before I go in is going to make all the difference.

"That is, if you want me."

"I do, definitely."

He grins. "It's a date."

Wednesday comes so fast I think I might have whiplash from it. I don't know where the time goes, but suddenly I'm in a suit, on the highway, with Ian driving me to my interview and I'm just sure I'm going to tank it.

"You're going to do great," he says, dropping his hand on my knee, squeezing. I take a shaky breath and nod, mentally going over my materials for the fiftieth time.

I've spent the past few days putting together a mock plan for what I'd want to do in Lyrett County if given the chance. There's still plenty of room for things to change, for plans to be altered, but I'm proud of what I've come up with. It's progressive and cost-effective, while pushing for more community activities and moving toward a greener city.

I don't know at all if it's what they're looking for, but if it is, I've probably got a pretty good chance.

"This doesn't seem like too much, does it?" I say, wrestling my pitch board out of the back of the truck cab.

"It seems like you care about getting this job," he answers.

"But that's good, right?"

He nods, kissing me and holding me there, drawing it out, letting his lips linger on mine. It has the desired effect, quieting all the anxiety and nerves bouncing around in my head.

"Knock 'em dead," he says, grinning.

I nod back. "Thanks for being here. I don't think I could face this alone."

Ian smiles. "You could, but I'm happy to be here. I'm happy you wanted me to come along."

I bite my lip before kissing him one more time for good luck. "Always," I say. "Okay, here goes nothing." I push my shoulders back, straighten my spine, and head toward what could very well be my future.

There's a cheerful receptionist that greets me, and she gestures for me to sit in the little waiting area where there are a few other hopefuls gathered. But none of them seem to have the amount of materials with them that I do, and I suddenly feel very self-conscious about how much prep work I've put into this interview.

I'm going to look like I'm trying too hard. Like I'm desperate. No one wants desperate.

"Mr. Rainier?" someone who's not the receptionist calls from a door behind the desk. I straighten up quickly and smile at her.

"Right this way," she says, smiling back. So far so good.

I'm brought into a room with half a dozen people around

a table and made to sit on the opposite side from them all alone. They're all looking at me expectantly and when one of them asks why I want this job, I know I'm going on too long about my aspirations and goals. I know I'm probably getting soap-boxy, but I can't seem to stop myself. And then without prompting, I pull out my project board, launching into examples and ideas I already have.

I do it all without watching them for feedback because I know the moment I pause for a breath I'm going to panic and not have any idea what I was just saying.

So I just ramble on and on for who knows how long, sure that I'm bombing this whole thing but unable to stop myself.

And finally, *finally* I run out of things to say and chance a glance at the panel of interviewers, expecting to find them already on the phone with security, trying to get me escorted out.

But instead they're looking at me with smiles and nods. An older lady in the center leans forward, her smile bigger than the rest.

"You know, we haven't seen anyone come in with this level of preparation unique to our town. So many people are coming in here and giving us generic pitches, but not one has addressed the particular challenges and needs of our community the way you have."

I'm left standing there speechless, not really sure how to respond.

"We technically have to conduct all the interviews we've scheduled," she goes on to say, "but I'm comfortable in saying I think you'd be a great fit here and I look forward to the chance to work with you. If you accept."

My eyes go wide and I hold on to the back of the chair in front of me since my knees are trying to buckle. But I manage to keep most of my reaction under wraps and give a professional nod.

"I look forward to it as well," I say, not even sure where the words are coming from. Thank goodness for autopilot, I guess.

"We'll be speaking to you soon, Mr. Rainier," she says, standing to shake my hand.

I shake hands all around and thank them again and then get the hell out of there before they can change their minds or I can screw it up.

I try to keep a straight face, thinking I'll play it cool with Ian until I have an official offer, but the moment I'm back in his truck he looks at me expectantly.

"How'd it go?"

Instantly I crack a smile that I can't hold in.

"It's not official until they do all the other interviews, but they offered me the job!"

His eyebrows shoot up and it takes a minute, but he smiles and pulls me in for a kiss.

"Let's go out to celebrate. My treat," he says, starting the truck.

He takes me to a restaurant I've never heard of, but it's *fancy*. There's linen tablecloths and candlelit service even though it's only lunchtime. I'm sipping a glass of chardonnay, enjoying my salad and salmon, enjoying the attractive man across the table from me and the feeling of accomplishment that comes with achieving a goal I've been working toward for five years.

Yeah, everything's great right now.

"So, are you thinking about living close to work? It's a nice neighborhood, but a little pricey. Lots of restaurants, though."

I shrug. "I haven't really thought that far yet. I'll probably need your expertise in picking out a neighborhood."

He smiles, but it doesn't seem to go all the way to his eyes.

I'm not sure why, but I get the feeling that Ian's not as happy as he seems.

"I still can't believe it," I say, shaking my head. "What are the odds?"

His grin grows and he leans across the table to kiss me. "I'm not surprised at all. Who wouldn't want you?"

I'm not sure I'll ever get used to him saying stuff like that. I blush and look down, poking at my salad. Out of the corner of my eye a flash of light catches my attention, but when I look up, I don't see anything. Maybe just lightning in the distance, or someone's watch glinting in the candlelight. Maybe it's nothing at all and I'm just trying to distract myself from the weird feeling settling in the pit of my stomach.

Throughout lunch, we talk a bit more about life in the city and all the things I have to look forward to.

It's not until we're back on the road to Umberland when I finally put my finger on what seemed wrong: through all our conversations of living in the city, Ian never once mentioned himself in my future. It's like he's already ready to move on once I leave town.

I don't want to, but I can't help but feel foolish. I feel like I should have known better. I shouldn't have thought things could be different just because it's me. He's still Ian, he's still the love 'em and leave 'em type.

Why should I be surprised? It's just a summer fling. We both knew I'd be leaving Umberland at the end of summer. What did I expect?

"Do you want to come back to my place?" he asks as we ride through town. I shift in my seat and shake my head.

"It's been a long day. I think I just want to go home."

I can tell he's disappointed, but why? Because there are only so many more opportunities to fuck me before I leave and he's missing out on one of them?

He pulls up outside of my parents' house and I know

there's some tension between us and I know it's my fault. Everything was fine before I started trying to analyze him.

"I'm really proud of you," he says, squeezing my hand.

I squeeze back, tears pressing at the backs of my eyes. I don't know what's wrong with me. Why this feels like good-bye. But it does, even though it's a happy moment.

"Thanks."

"I'll see you tomorrow?"

I nod, getting out of the car only to see him leaning over for a kiss. Guilt gnaws at me, so instead of just going inside, I walk around to the driver's side of the truck and give him the kiss he didn't get. "Tomorrow," I say.

And then I head inside. I go straight upstairs, needing time alone to think and regroup. To reassess what I want out of this and what's really important to me.

By the time I'm in bed and nearly asleep, I decide I just need to talk to him instead of playing guessing games. I need to know what Ian's thinking about me moving to the city and what that might mean for our future, or if he even wants one.

Even though there's still plenty of uncertainty swirling around in my head, I feel better for having a plan.

IAN

*A*fter dropping Grant off, I go back to the camp. But I sit around there bored and lonely and wallowing in my own self-pity enough that I eventually find myself at Barb's downing most of a pitcher of beer on my own.

It's not that I'm not happy for Grant. I am. I'm so happy for him. I know how much this job means to him. I see the way his face lights up when he talks about his dream career and I know this is a *huge* deal. He was hoping to get in on the ground floor and work his way up, but he's already got his foot in the door much higher up than that.

So of course I'm happy for him. I'd be a complete asshole if I weren't.

But it also means that he's going to be leaving. He's going to move out of Umberland and go to the city three hours away.

Long-distance has never really been a thing I've known how to do. When I was in the league, I basically just had a booty call in every city. Everything was much easier that way.

And I know three hours isn't *that* far, but it's far enough.

It's far enough that I won't be able to wake up with him, or fall asleep with him, or pick him up from work for a spontaneous dinner date.

Because those are the things I want to do with Grant. Along with so much more. I want to do the dumb, everyday, boring domestic stuff.

But I can't go back to the city. I can never move back there after everything that happened. There are too many painful memories there. Too much potential to run into people from my past that could make my life hell all over again.

And not just mine this time, but Grant's too.

I want to find a way to make it work, I really do. But I'm a realist. I know how these things go. And I'm worried that it's just not going to work. I'm worried that I'm going to lose him before I ever get the chance to see how far this could go.

"Can I get another?" I ask, waving my tumbler at Barb. I still hate that this is the only bar in town and I've got to patronize some homophobic jerk, but I need a drink or five right now, so where else am I going to go?

Besides, it could be worse. She doesn't refuse service to Trevor or anything. They just have a... tense relationship. Maybe there's more to it than just his *lifestyle* choices, I don't know. He did say something about family drama, not that I remember Barb being a part of his family.

But there's too many Rainiers to keep track of, so I wouldn't even be surprised if she is.

She pours another healthy measure of Jameson into my glass and I'm just bringing it up to my lips when my phone rings. I down the shot quickly, expecting it to be Grant, expecting to need the liquid courage. But it's not Grant, it's Mila, my old agent. I frown. I haven't heard from her since I retired. Not much reason to hear from an agent when you no longer have a career.

But if she's calling me now, that means… Well, I don't know what it means because she shouldn't be calling me.

"Hello?" I answer, almost expecting someone else entirely.

"Ian! Have you checked social media recently?"

"You know I don't bother with that shit," I grumble. Most of the drama surrounding the rumors about me and my retirement all happened because of fucking social media. It's a cancer on society if you ask me.

"Well, you should take a look," she says. "Give me a call if you need anything."

That just makes me frown deeper and I look at my phone like it's from another planet as she hangs up. I don't know if it's the alcohol or what, but that conversation was really confusing.

But then I heed Mila's advice and open up Twitter. It doesn't take long for me to see the links, to read the stories, to see me and Grant plastered everywhere on the internet with me leaning over the table to kiss him.

As far as the world at large is concerned, I'm still not out in public, but speculation is everywhere. Everyone's got their own theories, everyone's got their own bit to say about it.

And even as I'm reading through it, updates are happening, more stories are being posted—ones with corroboration from my teammates, people talking about the suspicions they had all along, how they were always okay with it even though they knew.

One article even suggests that I quit baseball because the stress of "living a lie" was too much and affecting my performance on the field.

Fucking ridiculous.

No one mentions how they basically drove me off the team. How they made me feel so unwelcome that I'd rather just leave the game than deal with the backlash of being who I am.

I shove the phone in my pocket after turning it off. I don't need to read any more of that shit. It's just going to make me angrier and there's nothing I'm going to do about it, so it doesn't matter. No point in being angry, now is there?

Not that being rational is going to stop the boiling anger simmering just below the surface, but a shot helps cool it down. Two shots has me to the point that I can laugh at those assholes and how quickly they fall over themselves to lie about who *they* are to look a certain way. They weren't *actually* supportive, but hell if they'd want anyone to know that.

Hypocrites.

By three or four I've lost count, and it really doesn't matter. I'm gonna have to sleep in my truck now, but Barb's nice enough to give me a pitcher of water since I promise I'll leave it by the door in the morning.

She's not all bad, I guess. Though I wonder if she'd have done the same thing if she knew who I'm dating.

I drink half the water before I pass out in the back of the truck cab. I drink the other half when I wake up at the crack of dawn, not that it does much at all to get rid of the angry throbbing in my head. Used to be I could drink like that any day of the week and wake up fresh as a daisy the next morning. Not anymore. I'm an old man now and having a handful of shots after I'd already had a pitcher and then some... Well, let's just say I can't hold my liquor the way I used to.

I stagger out and leave the pitcher by the door, just like I promised, but getting up was definitely a mistake. My stomach's sloshing with all that water and I feel like I'm in one of those hamster wheels at the end of a carnival fun house.

Shit.

The bushes by the door get the worst of it as I puke up that whole pitcher of water, my stomach still heaving long after its contents are empty.

"I'm never drinking again," I groan, wincing at the sun.

But I know that's a lie. This will definitely keep me away for a while, but it's what everyone says when they're hungover. Because it's torture, but we're all still crazy enough to subject ourselves to it for whatever reason.

My reasons don't seem all that great in the light of day, but just remembering the pictures of me and Grant all over the celebrity and sports news sites makes my blood run hot again.

I wonder how he's handling this. I turned my phone off last night so if he tried to call me he couldn't have gotten through. Damn, that was stupid. When I turn the phone on, there's about a hundred notifications, but none of them are from Grant. From the looks of it, they're all reporters, probably wanting to go through my whole life with a fine-toothed comb.

Well no thanks. I know it's a lot to ask, but I'd like to have *some* privacy now that I'm retired.

By this point my stomach's settled down, and now it would like me to know that it's *starving*.

These are the times I *do* miss living in the city. Because I'd have a billion options for a quick breakfast and probably half of them would bring it to me, or at least not require me to get out of my car.

Nothing like that exists in Umberland, and the only place for miles that's open and serving breakfast is Sheryl's Diner.

As hungry as I am, I'm not walking into that potential firestorm in my current state. I don't know who knows about the incident in the city, I don't know how they feel about it if they know, if they blame me, if Grant's getting harassed by reporters like I am...

I don't know anything until I see him, and the chances of him being at the diner are slim. So I head back to the camp instead. I've got the kitchen operational now. I'll make some eggs or something. Eggs and toast. And coffee. So much coffee.

And a shower.

Maybe the shower should come first. I definitely need to brush my teeth after throwing up. So I guess I've got a whole plan to keep me busy until Grant shows up to work.

He shows up a little later than usual—okay, a *lot* later—and I was almost starting to think he might not show up at all. But then I hear him pulling up and I'm relieved, but I'm also annoyed. I haven't heard from him at all and he's late, and I'm just sure that this is going to end badly. He doesn't want to deal with the publicity and I wouldn't blame him. Not to mention the distance…

I'm pushing a wheelbarrow full of gravel, laying a path to one of the cabins, when he comes up to me.

"Hey," he says.

"Hey."

"Sorry I'm late… I've had a lot on my mind…"

"Yeah," I grunt, dumping the wheelbarrow over. "You're not the only one."

His brow furrows at that, his lips pursing. I rake the gravel out and he just stands there.

"Well, anyway… what are you doing?"

"Working," I say, picking the wheelbarrow back up, heading back down to the pile of gravel. He's following me the whole time. "I guess you're not doing that here anymore, huh?"

I don't look at him for his reaction, I just start loading shovelfuls of gravel into the wheelbarrow. One after another, dust filling the air with huge clouds that make my nose tickle and my eyes water.

"Could you just stop for a minute?"

"Can't. I'm losing my help, if you haven't heard."

"Can we just talk about—"

"No," I cut him off. I know he wants to talk about the articles and I can tell by the way he's acting that it's not going to be a good talk. So no, I don't want to participate. He can just save us both the time and anger and leave.

"What's wrong? You can talk to me," he says, stepping forward, resting a hand on my arm so I have to drop the shovel.

But it's a stupid question. He's seen the articles. He knows what's wrong. And I don't want to talk about it. I've already told him everything about the situation I needed to say. There's nothing more to say.

"Ian," he says, his voice pleading. "Come on, talk to me."

I look down at him into those clear blue eyes, the young, hopeful face, and I can't do it.

I can't drag him into this with me. And I can't fight this fight again. I'm done fighting.

"You're not my therapist, Grant. You're just the guy I'm fucking."

He drops his hand, his face hardening all at once. Even I can't believe I really just said that, but it's for the best. This is going to end one way or the other. It might as well end now before it gets messier and more tangled.

"Guess you didn't change so much after all, did you?" he says, the words barbed, his throat tight with emotion. I feel so fucking guilty. I want to reach out and stop him from leaving, but instead, I let him.

Let him leave angry at me. Let him not get dragged into a tabloid mud campaign. Let him go back to the city and build his life there and not have to worry about keeping his long-distance boyfriend happy.

It's for the best.

I tell myself that over and over and over again. Every trip I take with the wheelbarrow, I tell myself I'm doing the right thing pushing him away and keeping my distance.

I must make a hundred trips up and down the hill with loads of gravel, filling in two long paths all on my own before I'm damn near ready to collapse from exhaustion.

The pain radiating from every nerve in my body seems a fitting punishment. I ache so much that just getting to the bedroom of the cabin is a chore, and I don't bother to undress. I don't even bother to turn out the light.

But as tired as my body is, my mind is still awake, still telling me I made a mistake pushing Grant away. Still telling me I need to find a way to make things right with him. I don't know how. I don't even know if I really think it's a good idea, but I know that I'm not making any decisions before I have a good night's sleep.

Good luck with that.

GRANT

*I*t's a good thing that I know the roads back to my family's house by heart because I can hardly see a thing beyond all the tears.

So that's how it is. How it all ends. He doesn't even want to *talk* about it. He's not even man enough to say, *it's over*?

I swipe at the tears streaming down my face, but no matter how many I wipe away, they're always replaced by more. How could I be so *stupid?*

I really thought Ian meant it when he said he was serious about this, about us, about trying it and seeing where it went.

Apparently, it went only far enough to sleep with me a few times before the summer was over.

I don't get it. He made such a good case to Trevor. It's not like I'm some random guy he can forget about and never see again if he wants to keep his best friend. So what's happening?

It feels wrong. I don't feel like this is how Ian should be acting about this whole thing and it makes me not want to believe it's really over.

The farther I drive, the more and more it seems like it

really is something we still have to talk about and figure out. Maybe he doesn't want to talk about it right now. Maybe it's still too fresh and he needs more than a day. I don't know. Maybe it *is* over and I'm just fooling myself. But I'm not accepting him just dismissing us like that. I'm not saying that's an okay way to end our relationship. He doesn't get out that easy.

By the time I'm pulling up to my parents' house, the tears are dry and I feel a little better. Not a lot better, but a little.

I head inside and of course Scout is right there in the living room. She looks up, frowns at me, and comes over, looking at me intently.

"What's wrong?"

"What?" I back up, trying to look confused. Her freaking superpowers have never been fair. She has the most uncanny ability to see right through any kind of facade I try to put up.

"What's. Wrong?" she repeats, a little more slowly, like I'm hard of hearing or slow.

"N-Nothing." I choke out a lie, trying not to meet her scrutinizing gaze. She's not quite got the same power as Mom *yet*, but she's getting closer and closer the older she gets. I feel bad for any future offspring of hers because they're never going to get away with anything.

"Grant Killian Rainier," she says, her voice harsh and demanding.

"Why is it so hard for you to just accept what I say?" I'm still backing up, but she's following me every step, still watching my eyes, making it almost impossible for me to look away or hide anything.

"Because I'm your sister and I know you. I know what you look like when you've been crying and I know what you look like when you're trying to hide it."

"So you know I clearly don't want to talk about it," I say, cursing immediately.

"A*ha*! So there *is* something wrong."

"Scout, can we just not?" I ask, my voice putting all my weariness on display. I know it's still the early afternoon, but I just want to go upstairs and be alone in my bed. I want to feel sorry for myself for a little while. Is that so wrong?

"No, we have to," she says, blocking my exit. She might be a foot shorter than me and a hundred pounds lighter, but I know better than to underestimate her. I've seen Scout take out guys twice her size. "I know you don't *want* to talk about it, but it helps, right? So what is it?"

"It's *nothing*," I emphasize. "Nothing at all." Not anymore. Not since Ian just wants to throw it away and pretend it's nothing. Even if I am determined to talk to him to make it official, I'm not sure there's another outcome anymore.

And that does it. The floodgates open and Scout's persistence crumbles as she pounces forward to envelop me in a hug.

"It's Ian, isn't it?" she asks, sobs racking my body. I nod and sob harder, clinging to her even though it's such an awkward angle. Scout's always been the one I talked to about crushes. Well, crushes other than Ian. Because my crush on him was always too embarrassing, always too impossible.

It should've stayed that way.

"Okay. I'm going to put a frozen pizza in the oven, you're going to pick a movie, and we're going to raid Mom's wine rack. Sound like a plan?"

I nod, sniffling, wiping my eyes. There's not really much chance of me getting out of it at this point, and honestly, maybe being alone isn't the best idea. Scout's on my side. I know she's going to have my back and help me get through this.

We're halfway through the second movie of the night when Trevor comes in and takes off his boots, sniffing the air as he walks in.

"Did you guys make cookies?"

"And brownies," Scout answers.

"And sundaes," I finish, holding up my bowl of what's basically ice cream soup at this point. But truth be told, I'm feeling much better. It might be the bottles of wine we've split, or the *Kill Bill* double-feature. It might even be the mountain of carbs big enough to satisfy a hippo, but yeah, I'm doin' all right at the moment.

That's why having to pause the movie because Trevor's looming and scowling at us is kind of a buzzkill.

"What do you want? There's more in the kitchen," says Scout.

He ignores her and turns directly to me. "What happened?"

"What makes you think anything happened?" I snap back.

"'Cause it did. So tell me."

I roll my eyes. He always thinks he knows everything. I hate that he just so happens to be right in this one instance, but he's going to find out one way or the other.

"Your friend is being a dick," I say, trying to sound nonchalant about it.

"Is that it?" he asks.

"What?"

"What actually happened?"

"Not that it's any of your freaking business, but I went to talk to him and he totally blew me off, basically told me he's through with me and I should get lost. So there. Are you happy? You were right," I snap, the tears coming back, clogging my throat, making it hard to swallow and see through the blurriness.

"Did you ever think you might be overreacting?"

That comes out of nowhere and hits me in the chest, knocking the wind out of me.

"What? Did you not hear anything I just said? *He* told *me* to leave. It's not exactly ambiguous, Trevor."

"Why are you making such a big deal out of this?" asks Scout. "You're the one that said Ian would do something just like this."

"Exactly," I agree. "You warned me he was going to hurt me and you were right. So I guess you win."

He rolls his eyes and crosses his arms. "You're so stupid sometimes. Have you looked at the internet at all in the last two days?"

"Um…" I haven't. Other than checking my notifications for emails, I've been too busy just trying to figure out what I'm going to do with Ian. And then gathering my courage to talk to him. And then being rejected by him. Then having an old-fashioned man-hating slumber party with my sister to get over him… So, no. No internet.

"What does that have to do with anything?"

Trevor groans like this is the most difficult thing he's ever had to explain. "Just Google his name."

I've got no idea what he's getting at, but he's serious enough that I pull out my phone and do what he says.

And the moment the search results show up, my stomach drops. My heart clenches and everything spins. It's the two of us, bright neon letters smeared across asking *GAY?!*

I don't even care. I'm not embarrassed by being caught in public. But I know what this means for Ian. I know how having his teammates find out randomly messed up so much for Ian. I can only imagine how shaken he is about this whole thing now. He's not out to the world still, and if he ever does decide to come out publicly, it should be on his time, on his terms. It shouldn't happen because someone's outing him against his will. It's just wrong. It's such a huge violation. And I feel terrible that he's going through it all over again.

But it gets worse.

It's not just the speculation that he's gay that's in the stories. It's comments from his old teammates, the people he talked about before. Comments saying how they supported him and his sexuality, that they were sad to lose such an important part of the team and it didn't matter to them at all even though they'd known all along.

I actually squeeze my phone so hard while I'm reading that that I'm afraid I'm going to crack it. How can they say those things and still sleep at night? They're just straight-up lying about how they treated him to make themselves look better. It's sick and disgusting and I can't let them get away with it.

Someone needs to tell the other side of the story.

"Why hasn't anyone called me for my side?" I ask suddenly. Scout's been reading on her phone too, Trevor hovering behind the couch looking over our shoulders.

"Everything I'm seeing calls you an 'unidentified male,' so maybe no one knows who you are yet?"

As much as I want to tell the other side of the story, the side where Ian was persecuted and mistreated instead of welcomed with open arms, I don't think I should do it without talking to him. It's probably for the best that I'm not being hounded by reporters.

"Let's hope it stays that way," I say. When I'm ready to speak on his behalf, I can reach out.

"I wouldn't count on it," says Trevor. "Those people can be vicious."

"What are you going to do?" asks Scout, resting her phone in her lap.

I shrug. "I don't know. I'm not doing anything until I talk to Ian."

"I thought you were mad at him?"

"That was when I thought he was being an ass about the job offer. Now I realize he's got more going on. I wish he would have talked to me about that too, but that's less of an issue right now."

"What job offer?" Trevor butts in.

"Grant's already got a job in the city!" Scout says excitedly.

"But don't tell Mom," I plead. "Not yet, at least. I need to butter her up first. And before that, I need to deal with this."

"You sure you don't have too much on your plate?" he asks, arching an eyebrow, giving me that stern judgmental older brother look I know all too well.

"Maybe I just need to find a way to make my plate bigger," I say.

He frowns, shaking his head. "That's not how that—"

"You should clean up before you go see him," Scout offers. "So you don't look like you've been crying all day."

"Good point," I agree, pushing out of my blanket nest, a new sense of purpose taking over. Ian needs me. He needs comfort and support and he needs to know that it's all right, that we're all right that this isn't coming between us.

I don't know what he was thinking earlier, whether he thought I was freaking out about the pictures or the articles, or the job, or everything? I don't know. But that's why we need to talk.

And we need to keep talking. We can't keep doing this. If we're going to try to make this work—for *real*—we need to communicate or we don't have a chance.

"Thanks for the heads up, bro," I say, clapping him on the shoulder as I skirt past to run upstairs for a shower. I don't care how late it is or even if he's already in bed. I'm still going to show up and support and comfort him. He's going to know I'm there for him and he's just going to have to deal with it, even if it is new and unusual for him.

IAN

*T*here's no way sleep's happening with so much running through my head. If it weren't for the lack of proper lighting, I'd probably be out doing some work just to keep busy. Not that my body much likes the idea of moving after the punishment I've given it today.

And I don't want to turn on the phone or the TV or anything else. I don't want to run the risk of seeing the same bullshit pushed in my face. Luckily for me, there's not much temptation. Cell signal out here is pretty awful and I haven't gotten the satellite hooked up yet for the TV. The guy should be here next week to install it, but for now, it's just me in the dark with my thoughts.

It's not a pretty sight.

And when I see headlights sweeping up to the cabin, I'm in such an exhaustion-induced delirium that I'm sure it's some overzealous reporter come to beat down my door until they get answers. I reach for the nearest thing on the top of my toolbox—a crowbar of all things—and brandish it like a bat. Time to show them what the best RBI in the division really means.

The footsteps that come up the walk aren't hesitant at all; they're sure even in the dark. I reposition my hands, my grip slipping with the dampness on my palms. They stop at the door, and where I expect a knock, the door just starts to open. There's not much light outside, but I've been sitting in the pitch black long enough for my eyes to be completely adjusted. And there's no mistaking Grant, even if the only light in the entryway is the glow of the microwave's clock.

The crowbar clatters to the floor in an instant and he steps forward, so close I can smell the clean springtime scent of his soap. I close my eyes, taking a deep breath of that scent. Then his arms are wrapping around me, enveloping me in a hug that I feel down to my very soul.

The warmth and compassion in that hug shatters something in me and I hug him back just as hard.

"I'm sorry, Grant. I'm so fucking sorry." I cling to him, refusing to let him go now that he's in my arms again. There's no reason for him to be. No one should have come back to me after the way I treated him, but he did and I feel like the luckiest asshole in the world.

"Shhh, everything's going to be okay," he whispers in my ear, stroking the back of my neck.

"Why—"

He shakes his head. "I didn't know about all the tabloids when I came to see you. I thought you were lashing out about the job offer…"

"So you weren't coming to tell me you were uncomfortable with the attention and couldn't handle being with someone in the spotlight?"

He rolls his eyes and pokes me in the chest. "You really do have an enormous ego, you know."

"You say that like I haven't had that exact reasoning delivered to me before."

"By me?" he counters.

"Touché," I sigh. "I'm sorry I was such a dick."

"So you're not second-guessing us?" he asks, and the vulnerability in his voice tells me so much. God, I'm an idiot. How could I have ever thought I could give this up?

"Hell no. That article shook me, but it's not you. You're fucking perfect."

He gives me a sly little smile and I'm sure he thinks he can hide that blush from me, but he can't. I see it. I love it. I might even lo— Well, one thing at a time.

"So what are we going to do about the job offer, then? Or living in the city?"

I sigh, holding him tighter, pressing a kiss to his temple. I can't believe I've got this guy in my arms, that I'm lucky enough to call him mine and I was almost stupid enough to throw that away. Never again.

"I don't know yet. But I want you in my life, and if you want me in yours, we'll figure it out together."

He grins, rocking forward on his toes to kiss me. "Sounds like we'll figure it out together, then."

Even though we're still in the dark just beyond the front door, I can see Grant looking around and frowning.

"Were you awake when I got here?"

I shrug. "Couldn't sleep."

He smiles, nudging me with his hips. "Think I could help with that?"

"What are you suggesting?"

His fingertip slides down the front of my bare chest slowly and he shrugs innocently. "Oh, just that you might sleep better with someone else in your bed. I've heard it can help some people."

"I see," I growl, gripping his lean hips, stroking my thumbs over that crease where his leg meets his pelvis, dragging it *close* to his groin, but definitely not close enough. Still, it's enough that I feel him growing harder against me, and it makes me hard in turn. God*damn* he never stops having this effect on me.

"Yeah, that's all," he says, breathless, his eyes heavily lidded.

"Because I thought you might be making some reference to the stereotype about men falling asleep after sex," I say, doing my best to sound innocent all while I'm getting closer and closer to stroking him through his pants.

He sucks in a breath and for just a moment, his eyes flutter closed completely. I lean in and kiss him, sucking on his bottom lip, swallowing the moan that rumbles from his throat as I do.

"I… I don't know why you'd think I'd suggest such a thing," he pants, his hands skimming down my abs, following the fuzzy patch of hair from my navel down under my shorts. He doesn't stop until he's cupping my erection in his palm, his thumb swiping back and forth over the head of my cock, spreading my precum around until everything's deliciously slippery.

"You're right," I say, sliding my hands away from his groin, actually pulling away from him entirely to offer my hand. He's pouting, and my dick's not happy about the loss of his touch, but I know this kind of teasing drives him crazy, and watching him lose his mind only drives *me* crazy. Win-win all around.

"Let's go to bed for an innocent night of above-the-shirt touching only."

He looks at me like I'm from another planet. "Now you're just being unreasonable. You're not even wearing a shirt."

"Oh, shit. You're right. Guess I should put one on." I grin and then he smacks me playfully, making me laugh outright.

I don't know how things can change this fast, but I guess that's what happens when two people really want something to work. Once we both got our heads out of our asses, at least.

"If you do anything with your clothes other than take them off, I'm leaving," he says, taking my hand. He walks close enough behind me to reach around with his other hand, stroking me again as we walk to the bedroom.

That walk alone is nearly torture for me. Not just because Grant's hand is driving me crazy, but because I worked myself so damn hard earlier today. Every time I've ever pulled that kind of stunt I've regretted it, and yet time and time again, I find myself taking my aggression out on my own body and paying the price for it later.

Now that price is going to be that I can't do all the things to Grant that I want to.

"Did you hurt yourself again?" he asks as we get to the bedroom.

"What?"

"You're limping and your whole body is really stiff."

I grin over my shoulder. "You never complained about my stiffness before."

He laughs and smacks me playfully again. "I'm serious. I know your body—" As if for emphasis, he strokes me from root to tip, with *just* the right amount of pressure to make my knees go weak. Of course when that happens I have to rely on my own strength to catch me, and in my current state, that just means I end up wincing the moment my knees buckle. "—And I know when something's not right with it."

"Just me being stupid," I say with a shrug. He strokes me again, and this time my eyes roll back. He's going just slow enough that I'm not going to get anywhere close to coming, but he's doing everything so *perfectly* that every stroke feels like I'm damn close.

"What'd you do?"

"Laid the gravel for cabins five and six."

His hand stills. "All of it?" he whispers. "By yourself? *Today*?"

I shrug, but even that hurts.

"Come on," he says, taking my hand, dragging me away from the bedroom. I have no real choice but to follow him even though that bed sounds like the best thing in the world. Especially with him lying next to me stroking my cock like that…

"Where are you taking me?" I whine.

He laughs and the sound is literally music to my ears. I was so convinced I wouldn't hear it again. That I'd lost him for good. "Don't worry, you big baby, I'm going to make you feel all better."

"Is that a promise?"

He leads me into the bathroom, turns on the shower all the way, and starts pulling my shorts down. "Have I ever disappointed you?" He crouches down in front of me and strokes my cock until I'm rock hard again. He leans forward, opens his mouth, licks his lips, and looks up at me as he slowly wraps them around my cock. He moves his head down, down, down, until I feel the back of his throat. I feel his muscles working as he fights against his gag reflex, and holy shit, it feels so good. He flattens his tongue against the underside of my shaft and I reach out to the wall for support, my head swimming with pleasure. I feel my balls start to tighten, the waves building inside me, pushing me closer to that place of pure bliss.

Grant draws his lips back, his tongue slipping around me in ways that have me seriously doubting he's as inexperienced as he says. Holy shit.

"I think the water's warm enough," he says, pulling back, standing up, stripping in front of me. But it's not a show this time. He's all business as he strips down and drags me into the shower with him.

It's not really meant for two people, but I'm not complaining about being so close to him.

Steam surrounds us, and he turns me so that the stream of water hits my tired and sore muscles. Meanwhile, he's got a washcloth and soap and he's gently—and *thoroughly*—cleaning me from head to toe.

Well, not quite. He drags the rag down over my shoulders, across my chest, working his way all the way down to my waist before he squats down to start working up from my toes.

I don't even care that he's teasing me and making me crazy with anticipation. Having Grant touch me is so fucking nice. Just being here in the shower, with the warmth relaxing my aches and the man I'm falling for taking care of me... Seriously, what could be better?

He puts the washcloth down and soaps up his hands real good, sliding them up and down my cock, over my balls, down, around my taint and...

"Oh *fuck*," I groan as his soapy finger slides up into my ass. My balls contract instantly and I claw at the tile wall, but I hold back. I have to hold back, because I know this is just the appetizer. I know there's more where this is coming from. Wherever the *hell* this is coming from.

He slides his finger in and out of my ass, massaging me from the inside, driving me absolutely crazy, making me exert every last bit of willpower I have. Seriously, watching Grant while he fingers me like this... I'm not sure there are many hotter things.

Just when I'm about to hit the point of no return, he pulls back, stands up, and smiles at me.

"My turn." He turns around and I growl the moment I realize what he's saying.

"Who are you and what have you done with innocent little Grant Rainier?"

"I've been corrupted by an older man," he says, thrusting his ass toward me.

I'm still hindered by the soft cast on my right hand, so I rely on my left to get the job done in the water.

I slide my hand down over his ass, squeezing his cheeks one at a time, spreading them, running my fingertip along his crack down to his little puckered hole. Making sure I'm good and soapy first, I slide two fingers inside of him.

"Ian!" he gasps, his muscles clenching and unclenching, trying to accommodate my fingers. I just leave them there for a moment, listening to his breathing, listening to the soft, moaning breaths as his muscles relax and he sighs, sinking back into me.

"Did you just use this whole shower as an excuse to get me to stretch your little asshole?" I ask, my voice a deep rumbly growl. Grant shudders and looks back at me with an insincere glare.

"I brought you in here to make you feel better," he says innocently.

"I definitely feel better," I groan, moving my fingers in and out of him slowly, slowly enough that he's trying to move his hips back to fuck them. Every time he pushes back I pull them farther away, and soon he's just resting his ass against me and my fingers are gone.

"So greedy," I mutter, rubbing my hand up and down his spine, rubbing my cock over his tight asshole.

This time, it's Grant that pulls away, straightening up and grinning at me.

"Not in here," he says, picking up the rag again to rinse any remaining soap residue off of me before he turns the shower off.

"What are you planning?"

"It really kills you to not know something, doesn't it?" He laughs.

"No… Not usually." But I want him. And I want him now. And he's teasing me. That's my job. I'm the one that does the teasing.

As he's toweling me off, he lingers to massage my shoulders down to my biceps.

"I never knew you had magic hands," I grumble, melting under his touch.

"I'm sure I'm not as good as the massage people you had in the league."

I shrug. "I'd rather you touch me any day."

He works his way down my body, massaging the knots and tightness out of my muscles as he goes. By the time he gets to my calves I'm the most relaxed I've ever been.

I'm also hard as steel.

He takes my hand again, draws me back to the bedroom, over to the bed, and gently nudges me to lie down.

"I've been thinking about this for the longest time," he says, climbing on top of me, straddling me, leaning forward to kiss me.

I'm loving this take-charge version of Grant, especially in my current state. I'm so tired and sore and I want him so much. I don't want to have to do any of the work, but I can't not have him.

I reach above my head to the nightstand by the bed. There's a drawer with condoms and the bottle of lube that I took on the kayaking trip. Grant takes it from me, kisses me again, his tongue forceful and hungry, making me dizzy. I'm not used to being on this side of things. I'm not used to letting myself be vulnerable.

He quickly sheaths my cock, then pours the lube into his hand and then smears it all over my throbbing length, his hand slipping up and down, the squelching sound only drowned out by my own grunting.

"I want you inside of me so bad," he says, lifting his hips, angling himself on top of me. And then he's sliding down. It's slow, but he's so tight, so warm, so *perfect*. Everything in my mind is blank other than the feeling of Grant sinking down on me.

"Be careful what you wish for," I growl, grabbing his hips, pulling him down the last inch in one hard thrust.

"Oh God, Ian…" he pants, his hands on my chest, his eyes closed tight, his mouth open in a silent cry.

"This ass is mine," I growl, thrusting up into him. "*You* are mine. Don't you ever forget that."

"I won't," he cries, lifting his hips on his own, slamming down again and again. "I'm yours," he screams. "I'm all yours. Fuck, Ian…"

There's nothing but the sensation of me inside of him, of the warm comfort that only comes with being deep inside someone you care about as much as I care about Grant. I never thought anything could ever feel this good, but Grant does. Everything with Grant feels good, and I never want it to end.

I watch his face twist and contort into the strange expressions of lust and pleasure. God it's sexy. I'm sure he'd hate it if he saw it, but knowing that I make him lose all control, that he's just fucking me with wild abandon and mindlessly seeking pleasure, it's more than I can take.

"I want you to come for me," I say, reaching between us to stroke him, matching his pace as he rides me. And it just magnifies everything. Everything just feels so good. I'm touching him and he's riding me and I'm inside of him and he's so lost to the ecstasy of it all…

"Ian… Oh, Ian…"

"That's it. Come for me, Grant. Come for me and I'll fill your tight little ass with all my cum. You want that, don't you?"

"Oh, fuck yes," he groans, his head thrown back as his ass

squeezes me tight. I stroke him faster and faster, feeling the effect of what I'm doing in the ripples around my cock. Every time I stroke my thumb over the crown of his cock, his ass squeezes around me, his muscles rippling and milking me.

"I'm going to—"

"You're going to come, because you're *mine*," I growl, stroking his cock and thrusting up into him at the same time. He sucks in a sharp breath and then his hot sticky cum is shooting out in spurts across my hand and my belly. The whole time there are echoes of his orgasm sending tremors through me, making every muscle in my body contract and focus on one point until I explode in a wave of the greatest nothingness ever. There's nothing but feeling *amazing*. No stress, no pain, no worries or insecurities. Just good feelings, my balls emptying every last drop until I'm completely spent.

"Oh my God," Grant purrs, snuggling close to my chest. I pull him close and just hold him there, my heart beating so hard and so fast I think it wants to join his. It almost hurts not to tell him all the things I'm feeling right now, but I don't think this is the right time. I don't want to demand too much out of this moment. It's already perfect the way it is.

"Yeah, I have to say I agree," I say, dragging my fingertips up and down the ridges of his spine.

"So we're going to make this work, right?" he asks, his voice full of cautious optimism and vulnerability.

"We are," I assure him. "I don't know what we're going to have to do to figure it out, but I know we will. I'm determined."

"Good," he says, stroking my chest idly. "I am too."

Then, after a few minutes of silence, he sighs. "You know I still can't sleep here though. Mom will be mad if I'm not home when she gets up."

I chuckle, kissing the side of his head. "Why does that make me feel like we're in high school?"

"But she's not doing breakfast at the diner today, so she won't be getting up until six or so," he says, grinning.

"What are you getting at?"

He shrugs. "Just saying, if you wanted me to stay, I could set an alarm. I know it's still not quite the same but…"

"You're crazy if you think I don't want you to stay every second you can."

Not that I can tell him at this moment, but sleeping with him, waking up with him, those are the kinds of things I've been dreaming about a lot lately. The kind of "relationship"-y things that I've never wanted to do with anyone else. With him, I want to do it all. I want to experience what it's like to have a boyfriend and to do the silly romantic things for each other.

I want to have a partner—not just a *partner*—and with Grant, I think I might have finally found it.

GRANT

I'm in Ian's bed, and he's working his way down my body with his mouth. He's trailing kisses lower and lower until he's kissing along my dick, blood rushing to meet his touch, me swelling in his hand as everything but this good feeling fades away into the background.

But somewhere, there's something in my head telling me to pay attention to it.

Even as Ian's mouth slips around me, I can't give in to the feeling because there's some nagging feeling in the back of my head, something telling me that this isn't quite right.

I groan as he takes all of me into his mouth, the feeling of him surrounding me like this almost too much.

"Grant Rainier!" A voice breaks through the haze of lust and pleasure. "Grant!"

It takes me a minute, but there's knocking too.

And then all at once the spell's broken and I'm blinking awake in my own bed, my cock hard as steel, but no Ian next to me.

I'd slipped back in a couple of hours ago and decided to try to catch a few extra winks before another busy day at the camp. I roll over, groaning, and sit up in bed, bunching up the blankets so my mother won't see my morning wood.

"I'm up, I'm up," I mutter, wiping sleep from my eyes.

The door bursts open and Mom comes in in a tizzy. I haven't really seen her like this before. She looks flustered and angry, but also worried? I don't know. Something's definitely got her worked up, and by the way she's looking at me that something is my fault.

"Have you seen this?" she practically shrieks, dropping today's paper in my lap. Apparently, Ian and my relationship is front page-worthy in Umberland.

"No," I groan, pinching the bridge of my nose. "I mean, I knew it was out, but I hadn't been identified by anyone."

"Why didn't you tell me you were dating Ian?" she says, actually sounding disappointed, maybe even hurt. I guess I was so preoccupied with my own concerns that I didn't think about how being left out of the loop might make Mom feel.

"I'm sorry. Everything's just been… complicated."

She frowns, her hands on her hips. "Well, it's not getting better. The whole world knows who you are by now and the house phone's already been ringing all morning."

I curse under my breath and she gives me a sharp look, but under the circumstances, I think even my mom can understand the necessity of strong language. As if to punctuate how bad things really are, my phone starts vibrating. I'd put it on silent once my alarm went off, and now when I pick it up I see over a hundred missed calls.

"I'm sorry, Mom. I should've told you. And I'm sorry if they badger you. I'll try to get this all sorted out."

Her expression softens and she pulls me into a one-armed hug, kissing the top of my head. "Are you sure you're handling all this all right?" she asks seriously.

I nod before I even have a chance to really think about it.

I don't have a choice. I have to handle it. For my family, for Ian, for everyone.

"I'm fine," I tell her. And it's true... Mostly. I'm not embarrassed at all by being outed or seen with Ian. I'm not ashamed of our relationship and I don't care if it's public, but I know that he does. So I'm worried about how he's dealing with this new twist. If he even knows.

"I'll be at the diner if you need anything. I unplugged the house phone though."

"Fair enough." I nod as she heads out, taking a deep breath before I start to listen to the voicemails.

Unsurprisingly, they're reporters. Some of them threaten me, some of them are demanding and rude. Some accusatory. Some making wild claims about Ian. After hearing the seventh entitled reporter tell me why I should give them an exclusive, I can't listen anymore. I delete them all. My blood's hot, my temper flaring.

Is this what Ian's been dealing with his whole career? Having to smile and play nice with these people?

Screw that. Screw them.

No sooner have I deleted every last message than my phone rings again. I'm ready to just bite the head off of the next person that looks at me the wrong way. I know I shouldn't answer for that reason, but having someone to lash out at sounds all right, so I answer.

"Hello?" Even mad, my voice sounds pleasant. I hate that. But then the voice that responds is so sweet and polite that I'm glad I didn't snap at her immediately.

"Is this Mr. Rainier?"

"Yes," I say cautiously.

"Thanks for answering," she gushes. "I'm sure you've been swarmed."

"That's an understatement; who is this?"

"Oh my gosh, I'm sorry," she says, nearly tripping over

herself. "My name's Samilla Ajiit and I'm a reporter for ESPN. I was wondering if you'd be willing to confirm the rumors that you're in a relationship with Ian Barrett?"

I grind my teeth. I don't know what else I expected, but I hate this. I hate people feeling like they have a right to know our private business, but there's only one way to make it go away.

"Yeah, I am," I say, hanging up the call before she can ask a follow-up question.

When I toss the phone down again, I'm shaking. Should I have done that? Should I have not said anything?

I snatch my phone up again and text Ian immediately, asking him if it's okay that I just told a reporter we're together, but he doesn't answer. I stare and stare at the phone, waiting a whole fifteen minutes, watching the clock. I'm waiting for his response, but it doesn't come.

Shit.

I can't just sit here and not know, so I jump out of bed, get dressed, and hurry down to the camp hoping I haven't just screwed up everything *again*.

Ian comes out to greet me, probably hearing my car come up the dirt road. The moment I'm out of the car he's wrapping me in a tight hug.

"I'm sorry you got dragged into this," he says, burying his face in my neck.

I cling back, my heart thundering against my ribcage. "Did you get my text?"

He looks confused and shakes his head. "I changed my number first thing this morning so they'd leave me alone."

I bite my lip, looking down at the ground. So he doesn't know. *Great.* I've got to find the courage to tell him *in person*. Beautiful.

"What's wrong?" he asks, reading me all too well.

I sigh. "I talked to a reporter this morning. They'd been

blowing up my phone and I was so sick of them so I just snapped at her and told her we're in a relationship without thinking. I know I should have talked to you about it first, but I—"

He pulls me into his arms and kisses me hard.

"You think I'd be mad that you told a reporter we're dating?"

I shrug. "You're not?"

"Well, we are, aren't we?"

I grin. "Yeah…"

"So what's there to be mad about?" He kisses me again and all the worries melt away.

"Why don't we both leave our phones in your car and ignore them all day?" he suggests.

"Sounds perfect."

We toss both the phones in the driver's seat and I lock the car where they're safe away from temptation.

As much as I'd like to, Ian and I can't just spend the whole day lying around enjoying each other's company. There's work to do, and a lot of it. But it's a good distraction and I love spending time with him.

With Ian at my side, I'm positive we'll weather this storm. The media will get bored and move on and we'll still have each other, which is more than I could have ever asked for.

IAN

We've been hard at work all day, and once quitting time rolls around, my stomach is growling. But the thought of making dinner sounds like one of the least pleasant things right now.

I turn to Grant, who looks about as tired as I feel. It was a good choice to leave the phones in his car, to forget all the nonsense of the outside world. It gave us time to spend the day together without any of those pressures. To just do our work and be together and not worry about anything else.

But now I'm hungry.

"What do you say we go to the diner for dinner?" I ask. It's spontaneous, but it sounds like a good idea and my stomach's definitely on board.

Grant doesn't look as sure, though. "Are you really ready to face that firestorm?"

I grin. "You really think *Umberland* is going to have a firestorm? Nothing's going to happen in our little hometown diner," I say, confident as ever about our sleepy town.

Grant doesn't look as sure as me, but he shrugs anyway. "Yeah, sure. I could use something in my belly."

I don't even have to ask him if his mom knows about us, because after being on the front page of the *Umberland Sun*, there's no doubt that *everyone* in town knows about us.

We take the truck into town and when we walk into the diner holding hands, we get a few looks, but no one says anything. No one's openly staring or looking shocked at all. For all my bluster, I wasn't really sure how the people of Umberland would react to us, but I'm starting to realize something. I'm starting to gain some perspective.

Umberland folks don't seem to care about my sexuality, and I don't have any plans to return to baseball, so what does it matter who knows I'm gay? I said I wanted to stop living a lie, and maybe that starts with *me* deciding I don't care.

"What are you smiling about?" Grant asks halfway through dinner. He's got the pork chop and mashed potatoes, I've got fish and chips, though he's already stolen three of my fries.

"Just thinking how much I like this. Just going out to dinner with you. Being your boyfriend," I say, grinning wider. It's still a little weird for me to say that, for me to be someone's *boyfriend*, but I do like it. A lot.

He smiles, poking at his mashed potatoes. "Did you ever think something like this would happen?"

"Did I think I'd go back to my hometown and find out that my best friend's gangly fourteen-year-old brother has grown into a sexy full-grown man, and then start *dating* that guy? No, the possibility hadn't really crossed my mind."

He laughs and nudges my shin under the table. "Well *I* thought about it. I had the biggest crush on you growing up. I mean, I never *really* thought, but obviously I hoped…"

"Guess you're luckier than you thought."

He rolls his eyes. "There's that ego again."

"You love it," I tease.

He gives me a flirty little smile as he leans forward and

sips his Coke. His face changes though, his eyebrows furrowing.

"What?" I follow his line of sight over my shoulder toward the windowed front of the diner. There's a crowd of people coming closer, and then before either of us can figure it out, the door slams open and a whole mob of reporters with cameras and microphones crowds into the tiny diner.

They home in on us right away and I stand up, ready to put my foot down.

"If you don't mind, I'm trying to enjoy dinner with my *boyfriend*," I growl, but instead of that having the intended effect of shaming them into backing off, me confirming things only sends them into another tizzy. They're shouting questions at me left and right and I can't even make any of them out because all the words are blurring into each other.

"Let's just go," Grant pleads, looking toward the door.

There's no way for us to get out the front with the way they're crowded around. They've got us trapped.

"Pssssst." It's Trevor from the kitchen, waving us over. Grant and I share a silent look and make a break for it. Before the reporters can follow us, the diner staff form a human chain and block them, securing our exit.

"You're lucky I was here," Trevor says, shuffling us toward the back while the rest of the staff keeps the mob at bay.

"We'd have found a way," Grant retorts.

"Now's not the time to bicker," I say, dragging Grant behind me to the back door. Luckily, we've all spent a ton of time in this kitchen. Sheryl's Diner hasn't changed in thirty years, so everything's exactly how I remember it.

I shove the back door open and the cool night air is a nice contrast to the sauna of the kitchen. But I'm not out two steps when there's a microphone shoved in my face.

"Ian, what response do you have to the allegations from Jack Alsworth?"

I was pushing right past her, but that stops me dead in my tracks. Accusations? I freeze, narrowing my eyes at her.

"What are you talking about?"

She must sense the rage simmering just below the surface, because she takes a step back, licking her lips nervously. Grant's still clinging to me from behind, but I feel him shuffle uncertainly, wanting to get out of here before the rest of the reporters get past Trevor.

This one is the only one back here, and she's a tiny thing. It wouldn't be hard to push past her, but I want to know what the hell she's talking about first.

"Um... Mr. Alsworth claims that you sexually assaulted him, and that the team, the coaching staff, and owners helped you cover it up by firing him."

It's such an absurd idea that I laugh right in her face. Absolutely ridiculous.

I grab Grant by the hand and pull him along behind until we get to my truck. The reporters are still contained within the diner, so we slip out without being seen. We're a block away before Grant says anything.

"What was that reporter talking about?"

I sigh, rolling my eyes. "Jack Alsworth. He was on the team for less than a season, never made much of an impression, really. Definitely never hung out with me or my circle. I barely even talked to the guy, and I definitely never came on to him or assaulted him. I'm in the papers for something somewhat controversial, so I'm sure he's just trying to get his fifteen minutes and drag me down at the same time."

Grant fiddles with his fingers in his lap. "Don't you think you should be more worried about these accusations?"

"No," I laugh. "They're complete bullshit. It'll fall apart before tomorrow morning, you watch."

He doesn't look convinced, but I'm having a hard time worrying about it. I've finally, *finally* after all these years been able to realize that it *doesn't matter*. What other people think or say about my choices, the judgments they make, the opportunities I might be denied—it doesn't matter. I'm not going to hide who I am anymore. I'm not going to let anyone intimidate me or shame me because of it.

Jack Alsworth is an idiot if he thinks these allegations are going anywhere, but he's an even bigger idiot for picking *me* to go up against.

GRANT

*N*ow that we're officially a couple and public, it feels so silly to be sneaking back into my parents' house every night and back into my room. I hate not spending the night with him, but Ian's trying to stay in my parents' good graces.

Which I guess is fair. I wouldn't want to end up on their bad side either, but I hate that he chooses *now* to be responsible. I bet if he didn't know my family the way he does that he'd be singing another tune, but that's always been the problem with being a Rainier. There's pros and cons and one of the cons is that *everyone* knows your family.

I get that he wants to be respectful, but I'm an adult and I shouldn't have to be waking up alone when I have a boyfriend I'd rather be waking up with.

Though I have to admit it is nice to come downstairs every morning to breakfast and coffee. Whether it's Mom or Dad making it, there's always someone behind the stove filling the house with delicious smells. This morning, it's Mom behind the stove and she looks at me when I come into the room, arching a brow.

"There's something for you on the front porch," she says cryptically.

I frown, looking toward the front door, not that that tells me a damn thing. I don't have x-ray vision, so I don't know what I'm expecting. Curiosity's gnawing at me, but so is the need for caffeine, so I make myself a mug before I head toward the door.

Something for me on the... I open the door, still trying to make sense of what Mom said. There's no package on the front mat, nothing glaringly obvious right in front of the door.

"Hi."

I think I jump three feet off the ground I'm so startled. I nearly drop my coffee and it sloshes over the edge of the mug, but I dance back just in time to avoid being burned.

"Oh God, did I scare you? I'm sorry," she says, standing up from the porch swing, her eyes huge and apologetic. She looks familiar—skin the same rich brown as my coffee, long straight black hair, dark hooded eyes, tilted at the corners. There's no one in Umberland that looks like her...

"You're the reporter from the diner last night," I accuse, backing up into the door.

She holds her hands up. "You also spoke with me on the phone. Samilla Ajiit?"

I remember her gentle tone in contrast with all the demanding rudeness in my voicemail box and I relax a fraction, but I'm not letting my guard down by any means.

"I was hoping you'd have a few minutes to talk?"

"Talk about what?" I growl, sipping my coffee, glaring at her.

"About Ian, first of all. Maybe your relationship? There are a lot of rumors swirling about him and it would be good to have his side of the story, or even the side from someone close to him."

I sigh. She's got a point. If there are accusations going around, Ian's silence is just going to make him look guilty and that's the last thing we want. So I sit down on the porch swing and she sits back down with me, smiling.

"Thank you so much," she says.

"I haven't agreed to anything."

Her smile fades a little, but it's back in a moment. It doesn't seem like there's much that could deter Samilla, but I admire that quality in a person.

"Okay, well, as I mentioned on the phone, I'm a reporter for ESPN. We got word of these allegations coming from Jack and—"

"What exactly are the allegations?" Maybe this is all some misunderstanding. Maybe this Jack guy is mildly homo-phobic and misread something as a signal or as getting hit on. Straight guys are always thinking gay guys are hitting on them. Maybe this could all be cleared up with a conversation.

Samilla licks her lips nervously, tapping her foot. "Well, the allegation is that Ian tried to force himself on Mr. Alsworth. In the current climate, no one's getting a pass with these kinds of allegations, so we're being pushed to investi-gate them as hard as we can. No one wants to miss the scoop. But I've been in sports reporting long enough to know when something stinks. Ian's always seemed like a stand-up guy to me, and Jack... Well, I probably shouldn't say anything," she says, giving me a sheepish smile.

I know this could all be some kind of trick, her just trying to earn my trust, but if that's the case it's working. She seems to genuinely be on Ian's side, and I feel like we can use all the allies we can get.

"The whole thing is ridiculous. Ian would never do some-thing like that. And it's this guy Jack's word against his. I'm sure truth will prevail."

Samilla gives me a look. A look that tells me she thinks

I'm being naive and stupid. Maybe I am. Maybe this is bigger than I'm giving it credit for.

I know Ian's not worried about it, but maybe he should be. There were a lot of reporters at the diner last night. That seems like a pretty big deal.

"Here's my card," she says. "I'd love to get his side of the story, and I really think the public should hear it too. For his sake," she adds, something grave and meaningful in her tone.

If nothing else, this reporter definitely thinks this is a serious issue, and that makes me reconsider my cavalier attitude.

"I'll see what I can do," I promise. She nods, and heads down the porch steps to her car. I wonder how long she was camped out here waiting for me. Long enough for Mom to be annoyed about it.

But she's the only one with the dedication to do that, and she does seem to believe in Ian's innocence, so maybe it's for the best that he talks to her. I'm definitely going to try to convince him.

When I get to camp, Ian's already painting the trim on the cabins. There are another dozen or so cabins scattered across the property, but our main goal so far is to get the handful up front next to his ready for people to rent or whatever.

"Hey, you," he says cheerfully from up on a ladder.

"Can you come down for a second?"

He doesn't argue, puts his paintbrush down, descends the ladder, and sweeps me into a kiss.

"You're right. I can't get out of my duties."

I can't help but smile even though I'm trying to be serious and have a conversation with him and he's being a goof.

"That reporter that cornered us last night was at my house this morning."

His arms stiffen around me, his whole body going rigid.

"I think you should talk to her," I continue. "There's a lot

175

going on and I think it would be good for the world to have your side of the story."

Ian's face tightens, his jaw clenches, and he shakes his head. "I'm not going to feed the gossip monster. They'll lose interest soon enough, believe me."

I shrug, trusting him. "If you're sure." I'm not going to push it. He seems very certain about this, and honestly, he has way more experience in dealing with this kind of stuff than I do. He's been handling the press his entire career. If he says we should just let it go, I'll take his word for it.

"I am. Why don't you grab a paintbrush and help me?"

And just like that, we fall into the easy rhythm of working together. By lunch, we've nearly finished painting all the trim on one of the cabins, even though it's taking two, sometimes three coats in places.

We head down to the lake for lunch at the picnic table, and then—as usual—he coaxes me out into the water. But I'm not really afraid anymore. I'm able to swim all the way out to him from the shore, even when he's far enough out that our feet don't touch the bottom.

And when I swim to him, he's there to reward me with a kiss.

"You've made so much progress," he says warmly, his arms around me, his hands splayed across my back.

"I've had a good teacher," I say, clinging to him, the warmth from his body seeping into me, making me want him like nothing else. "Thank you again, by the way... For being such a good teacher and helping me get over my fear. It's silly to have gotten this far in life without facing it."

He smiles. "You just needed a little motivation."

My face heats at his implication. Well, it's not *just* an implication, his hand is on my ass, squeezing. He kisses me, his lips molding to mine, his tongue teasing at the seam until

I part them. Instantly he's invading my mouth, making my head swim with the sensation and the raw need it creates.

He's grinning when he pulls back.

"What was that for?" I ask.

"A thank you of my own."

"Oh?"

He kisses me again, this time a quick peck, but his teeth drag across my bottom lip, sending shivers all the way to my toes.

"Yes, for helping me to get over *my* fear. The fear of being outed and living openly. Even though I'd resolved when I came back to Umberland to be open to love and all that, I still didn't have the courage to actually come out publicly. I was still living a lie. But being outed by the media—having you support me and be there for me—it made me realize whose opinions really matter and whose don't."

He's holding me so close and his words are so sincere and heartfelt that I nearly break. I nearly crack and tell him right here and now that I think I'm in love with him. But just as the words are about to leave my tongue, I reel them back in.

It feels too soon. And I'm still not sure what Ian will say. He might just think I'm feeling things more intensely because he's my first. But Ian's *always* been my first, and he'll always be the one I go back to, the one I fantasize about, the man of my dreams.

That's just even more reason to hold out, to not risk pushing him too hard when he's only now coming to terms with who he is.

"I'm so lucky to have you, Grant," he says, resting his forehead against mine.

"Ditto," I say, tightening my arms around his neck, holding him close, just drifting in the lake together like that. It's just about perfect.

IAN

*A*nnoyingly, three days later and the reporters still haven't gotten bored. It must be one hell of a slow news week, because they're crawling all over town, trying to find anyone to give them anything. What's surprising to me is how the town has reacted. I thought they might resent me for bringing all this attention here, but it seems that instead they're as annoyed with the outsiders as I am.

From what I've heard, no one's giving them anything. No one's talking to them, Sheryl won't let any of them eat at the diner, and even Ms. Giddons, crotchety old lady that she is, won't let any of them rent a room at her inn. Ryan's even taken to keeping an eye out so he can ticket any of them sleeping in their cars. So they've got nowhere to stay and nowhere to eat. They're not going to last long at this rate.

It's touching, really. I wouldn't have expected the town to rally around me like this, but I guess that's what you do when you're from a small town. Even if you may not fully agree with each other or support their choices, when it comes to outsiders, it's always us versus them. In this instance, it's working out in my favor.

So even though reporters are still crawling around my town, trying to take my picture, badgering my friends, I'm in a pretty good mood. I'm planning a trip into town for supplies before Grant and I get to work today, but as I'm heading to my truck, I hear tires coming down the road. He's early.

Not that I'm necessarily upset about getting to spend more time with him. I grin to myself and lean against the truck door, waiting for him to make his way all the way down the road. We'll just go shopping together. It's always fun to tease him in public.

But the car coming down the road isn't Grant's, and I stand up straighter, stiffening at the sight of the dirty white Crown Vic. I don't know anyone who drives anything like that, so it's got to be a reporter here to ruin my good mood.

"You're trespassing," I call to him as soon as he opens the door. But this guy doesn't look like a reporter. He doesn't have a camera or a mic. He's just got a folder. "You've got thirty seconds to get back in your car and leave before I call the cops."

He grins and I don't like it. He's got too many teeth, his face has too many lines, and he looks like the kind of leathery old man in a fantasy story that you shouldn't have made a deal with.

"Don't need more than thirty seconds," he says. "You Ian Barrett?"

I roll my eyes. "That's not exactly a secret."

He steps closer, holding the folder out in front of him. "You've been served."

Then, like he's afraid I've got some plague or something he's going to catch, he hightails it out of here, his ancient Ford leaving clouds of dust behind him.

"Served?"

The papers in the folder are full of a bunch of official-looking papers, covered with lots of long words I don't really understand, but I get the general idea of it.

Jack's fucking suing me. For "loss of livelihood, emotional damage, and collusion with team owners to damage his career and fire him."

It's complete and utter bullshit and I can't believe he found a lawyer to take his case.

I'm shaking, sitting in the cab of my truck poring over the papers, trying to make sense of everything, but I know I can't do this alone. I need help. I need a lawyer, but I need someone I trust. So there's really only one person to call.

"Ian?"

"Mila, hi, I…"

"What's wrong? You sound panicked."

"He's fucking *suing* me!" I roar, saying it out loud for the first time. Poor Mila. She doesn't deserve that, but she's my agent… was my agent, she's used to it.

"What? Back up, who's suing you?"

"Jack!" I huff.

Mila growls, actually *growls*, and I think it's the first time I've ever heard that sound from her. "You've got to be fucking kidding me. For what?"

"All this bullshit about me trying to 'force myself' on him. He's claiming I convinced the owners to fire him to cover it all up and hide me being gay."

"That homophobic self-centered piece of *shit*," she curses. I think she might actually be angrier about this than I am, and that's saying something.

"I've got this subpoena and I was hoping Perry could…"

"Yes, of course. We'll drive out there this afternoon and go over the whole thing in person. This is ridiculous, Ian, and we're not going to let him get away with it."

I actually let out a sigh of relief. Thank God for agents married to lawyers. After we hang up, I shove the folder into my glove compartment and head into town for those supplies. I can't let this keep me from getting my work done. I can't afford it if I want to get this place fixed up in any reasonable amount of time.

When I get back to the camp, Grant is actually there, and he looks worried as I get out of the truck. Does he know about the lawsuit? I groan inwardly. I really don't want him to know about that until I've got it all taken care of and out of the way. I don't want him to worry about it.

"I could have gone into town and gotten that stuff for you," he says as I get out of the truck.

"Why?" I laugh. I don't think he knows, so I'm just going to play it cool.

"Because… reporters?" he pouts.

I kiss him. "That's sweet, but you know they're just as eager to talk to you as they are to me. Besides, I think most of them are giving up at this point. Ryan scared a few of them off when he warned them about how people around here like to shoot unwanted folks on posted private land."

Grant snorts. "That sounds like Ryan."

"He's a pretty nice guy, he's been a big help this week with all these clowns."

"Yeah, I still don't understand how *he* was ever married to *Barb*."

I freeze. "No shit?"

He laughs. "I know, right?"

"That is a weird one."

"They've got a really cute little boy though, so I guess it's not all a loss. He's actually getting back to himself after the divorce."

"Maybe we should invite them to dinner once all this is done to thank him for keeping out the vermin," I suggest.

Grant nods. "I'm sure he'd like that. I know Troy would *love* this place. What five year-old wouldn't?"

"Guess we should get back to work then, huh?" I say, even though my hands are on his hips, holding him close. He pouts up at me.

"Do we have to?"

"Well… *no*…"

He sighs. "But we really should, I know. All right, let's get to it."

"You're not going to like this, but we really should work on the dock."

He makes a face, but eventually nods. "Yeah, I know. Other people are going to want to use it, even if I'm always going to be too chicken to."

"Are not. Jumping off the dock's not that much more of a step from swimming out from shore."

He looks skeptical. "It seems like a *huge* step. One might even say a *leap*."

"Ha ha ha."

We're still laughing and teasing as we get out to the dock, and it's almost easy to forget about everything that happened before he showed up this morning. But once we settle into a rhythm, it all comes rushing back. I start to think about that guy pulling up, handing me those papers, the legalese swimming before my eyes as I tried to make sense of what it was saying.

"You okay?" Grant asks.

"Huh? Yeah, why?"

"You've been prying that one nail out for three minutes and it's not in the wood anymore."

"Oh… Yeah." I lift the nail out and toss it in the designated bucket.

He lifts his eyebrows at me, smirking that knowing smirk that always annoys me because he sees more than he should.

"So, what is it?"

I shake my head, trying to smile to play it off. "Just

thinking about all the fun times we had jumping off this dock as kids. It'll be good to see kids playing on it again."

"Yeah…" he says, still watching me out of the corner of his eye even as he goes back to work. He's on to me and I don't blame him. I'm acting suspicious and I can't help it. I don't know why I can't just pretend that everything's okay, but I keep thinking about these allegations being taken seriously, my name being dragged through the mud, Grant and his family getting dragged along with me. The Rainiers *are* Umberland. There's so much more than just my reputation at stake, and I don't know how to protect them all.

I really hope Perry can nip this thing in the bud. Otherwise, I don't know what I'll do.

A dull thud sounds and Grant and I both freeze, but I know what's happened an instant before he does because my thumb *erupts* in pain.

"FUCK," I shout, the yell echoing out across the lake, stirring birds on the far shore. But all I know is that my whole hand feels like a giant ball of pain and my vision's starting to go blurry and dark on the edges.

"Oh no… That's the same… Shit, come on. Straight to the doctor," Grant says, crouching down, slipping his arm around my back, resting my good arm around his shoulders. He stands and pulls me up with him. I'm in no position to resist or complain. My brain is nothing but pain signals screaming back and forth at each other.

Pro tip: Don't smash your broken thumb with a hammer weeks after breaking it in the first place. It doesn't feel good.

I'm on the verge of passing out as Grant shoves me into the passenger seat of his car and I don't know why it hurts so much more this time than last time. I guess because it's already tender. I feel like I handled this better last time.

"Here, hold on to this, it'll help the swelling," he says, wrapping my unbroken fingers around the handle above the door. It's smart, keeping my hand elevated keeps the blood draining down, keeps it from throbbing and pooling in my thumb.

I wouldn't have thought of that right now.

I'm so lucky I have Grant.

"I'm never going to let you touch a hammer again at this rate," he admonishes, racing down the road. But I know he's just worried. I can see it in the set of his jaw and how he's gripping the steering wheel. I reach out with my left hand and settle it on his thigh, squeezing.

"Hey, it's just a thumb. I'm not dying, I swear."

He turns and looks at me, his eyes searching for a second. We've been through a lot the past week or so and I know it's taken its toll on him the same as it has me.

"I promise. I'm fine."

He nods and blows out a long slow breath, his body visibly relaxing as he does.

"I'm sorry I'm such a klutz and keep worrying you," I say, grinning through the pain.

"I'm just going to put you in a plastic bubble," he teases.

When we get to the clinic, we go through the same routine as last time, but this time Dr. Barnes is not nearly as friendly as she was last time. She's cool and detached, almost dismissive, and it's getting on my nerves. The last time I was here, she was all over me. Why? Because she thought I was available? Because she thought I was straight?

"There's no reason to treat me differently because I'm gay," I snap at her after coming back out of the x-ray room. She keeps sending these snide little smirks at me and Grant and I've had enough of people judging me or the people I love. I'm done with it. I'm done with apologizing for who I am.

"What?" she asks, frowning, taking a step back.

"You were a lot friendlier when you thought I was straight."

Dr. Barnes's jaw drops and she shakes her head. "Oh, no, it's not that. I was just surprised to learn you're gay. It makes complete sense now why you didn't want to go out with me."

I don't know why, but that just makes me angrier.

"It's not the only reason. I wouldn't date you even if I were straight," I snap.

Her eyes harden and she glances at the x-ray for just a second. "Your thumb will be fine if you stop ignoring my advice and manage to avoid injuring it again. Have a nice day."

She turns and leaves the exam room and Grant's just giving me this *look*.

"What?"

"Did you have to be like that?"

"Like what?"

"You were super hostile with her."

"I'm not going to let her think she can sit here and quietly throw shade at you. Like I didn't go out with her just because I'm gay. I didn't go out with her because I was already smitten with you *and* I'm gay."

He rolls his eyes, but he's smirking at me as he holds out his hand. "You're impossible, you know that?"

"But you like it, admit it," I tease.

He chuckles, shaking his head. "Heaven help me, I do."

"I'm really glad I never took those pain pills before. I don't think the doc's going to want to write me a script now and I could definitely use one."

He lifts his eyebrows. "Oh, so Superman is human after all."

I shake my head, rolling my eyes, kissing him. "Of course not. Superman is Kryptonian."

"And *I* got teased for being the nerd."

We head back to the camp even though I know there's not a chance in hell Grant's going to let me do anything else today. When we get back, there's another car up by my cabin, and even though I don't recognize it, I recognize the redhead sitting on the hood with her arms crossed.

"*There* you are!" Mila says the moment I climb out of the car. She comes right over and hugs me. "Where were you?"

I hold up my hand and my blackened thumb. She winces.

"That doesn't look pretty."

"Doesn't feel great either."

"I'll bet," she says, her voice still cheerful. "I'd ask for a tour of the place, but I assume you want to get right down to business?"

"Ian?" Grant asks from right behind me. My heart tightens and I instantly feel guilty for not telling him sooner, but there was no reason for him to worry.

"That guy making the accusations has decided to sue me," I tell him. He gasps, a hand flying up to cover his mouth, his eyes wide.

"Are you *serious*?" It's not shock in his voice now, it's pure indignant rage. That's my guy.

"Yeah, but Mila was my agent, and her husband Perry here is a lawyer, and we're going to figure out what to do about all this."

Grant nods. "I remember the name." I haven't done a lot of talking about my career, but there's no way to talk about it without mentioning Mila and all she's done for me.

"Perry, get out of the car," Mila calls, knocking on the window, shaking her head. "I swear he loves this thing more than me."

"Well, do *you* have a heated leather interior?" I ask.

She flips me the bird, smiling.

Perry gets out and takes a deep breath, looking around at

the campsite. "Shane would love this place, don't you think, Mi?"

"Let's go inside." Grant comes up, walking right beside me as I lead the way and I can tell he's mad.

"I'm sorry," I whisper. I should have told him sooner. He shakes his head.

"It's fine."

I know it's not, but at least we're not going to talk about it now, not while Mila and Perry are here.

Inside, I pour everyone a glass of lemonade from the pitcher Grant made a couple of days ago. He knows I like it, so he spoils me and makes some fresh every few days.

"So, I've reviewed everything pertaining to your case, Ian, and I think it's in your best interest to settle," Perry says, accepting the glass of lemonade with a grateful nod.

"What?"

"No!"

Mila and Grant both protest at once, but I don't say anything.

"Per, you don't know Ian like I do. He'd never do something like what this guy is saying. He doesn't have a leg to stand on."

Her husband doesn't look like he's swayed at all. He nods, like he understands everything she's saying, but she's still missing the point.

"I think what Mr. Alsworth is after is money. It doesn't matter if Ian is guilty or not. Settling is how we make this go away."

I'm inclined to agree with him. All I want is for this to disappear so I can move on with my life.

"But isn't settling just an admission of guilt? You have to fight this, Ian. You can't just let him win with these baseless rumors."

I can tell this is important to Grant. I can see the fierce

shine in his eyes that says he's ready to go out for blood. And I love that. I appreciate it so much. But I just don't know if it's appropriate this time.

I don't want to be labeled a pervert or a rapist. Gay people have it bad enough in this country without me adding that stain to our kind, even if it is all bullshit.

But I also don't want our whole lives to be open to public scrutiny. When the tabloids latch onto a story, they leave no stone unturned.

"Please, Ian? For us? Don't let him get away with this."

And then I see the other side of it. My name always preceded with "alleged rapist," Grant having to live with that, with explaining that. Or would he? It might be too much to deal with.

And what would ever happen if I wanted kids?

He's right and I know it. I can't let Jack drag me through the mud for his own gain. I can't just roll over and take it.

"All right. Let's do it. Let's fight him. Will you represent me, Perry?"

He sighs, shaking his head. "I think you're making a mistake, but I will."

"You better be as good as Mila says you are," I joke.

He chuckles. "Even better."

"Good," I say, thrusting my hand out. We shake and Mila gives me a hug before they leave.

"We'll be in touch," she promises.

And then it's just me and Grant alone in the cabin.

"I'm sorry I didn't tell you about it soo—"

"I think you should talk to that reporter now," he says. He looks determined, strong. This is the man I've fallen in love with. There's no denying it.

"I think you're right."

IAN

$\mathcal{I}$'m nervous the next morning when the reporter's car comes up the road to the camp. After talking about it with Grant, I called her and arranged a meeting. She wanted to come out and see what I've been up to since retiring, and she's even bringing a cameraman, which I'm not so sure about. But Grant keeps telling me I need to trust her and hope for the best.

"Are you sure you don't want me to hang around?" he asks, hugging me from behind as we watch her car approach.

"I do, but I think this will probably go better if you're not there. It's going to be hard enough to open up about things as it is."

He nods, kissing my neck. "I'm going to work on the stage, then."

I grin. "What, not brave enough to venture out to the dock alone?"

He smacks me playfully. "You know I'm not. You don't have to rub it in, meanie."

"Thanks for convincing me to do this," I say, kissing him

as he lets go of me. The reporter's car is coming to a stop, dust settling in the wake of her tires.

"Good luck," he says, giving me a little thumbs up before dashing off.

I rock on my heels waiting for her to get out, my whole chest filled with the nervous buzzing of a thousand butterflies. Was this a mistake? Putting it all out there for the world is such a huge step and I don't know if anyone's going to take my side, even after all of this. What if it's for nothing? What if Grant and I still can't be together because I'm labeled a pervert?

"Hi!" she says brightly, stepping out of the modest midsize sedan. In the city, it's a fairly average car. Out here it's so nice it might as well be neon green. She tucks a lock of straight black hair behind her ear and practically jogs over to me with her hand outstretched. "Samilla Ajiit, we spoke on the phone?"

I nod, taking her hand. "Ian Barrett."

She grins. "I know who you are, Mr. Barrett."

"Please, Ian."

"This is Howard, my cameraman. You can basically pretend he's not here."

I shake Howard's hand.

"Don't worry, I'm used to it," he says. "Also, I hope it's not inappropriate, but I've always been a huge Hawks fan and you're one of the best we've had out on the field since the '97 team that made it to the playoffs."

"Thanks man, that means a lot. If you want me to sign something later, I'd be happy to."

"Oh, really? That would be awesome. My kid, Joey, he's eleven and he's so upset about all this. Doesn't understand why people are being mean to you—"

"*Ahem*," Samilla clears her throat pointedly. "We do have

work to do, boys. We want to get Ian's side of the story out there, don't we?"

Howard and I both mutter, a little cowed by the admonishment, but I appreciate Samilla's dedication.

"I thought it would be fun to go around the camp, see what you've been up to, and use that time to try to scout a location for the main interview."

I already know the perfect spot. That picnic table by the lake, but I'm sure she'll find it easily too.

"Sounds good," I say, nerves swimming in my gut. They went away for a minute while I was talking to Howard, but now they're back in full force remembering how important this interview is.

"Just relax. We're having a conversation, no need to be tense," she says, smiling at me, her almond-shaped eyes sincere.

I blow out a long breath and chuckle. "That obvious, huh?"

"I know how it is." She smiles and makes a hand motion to Howard who lifts his camera up to his shoulder. I guess we're rolling.

"So, Ian, we know there are some questions about the circumstances surrounding your retirement, and we'll get to that a little later, but what have you been up to since you left baseball? Things have been awfully quiet from you."

I laugh and try to act like I'm talking to an old friend, or a fan, not a network of people who are going to judge me for crimes I didn't commit. "Well, I moved back to my hometown and took over the old camp I used to come to every summer as a kid. I've got a lot of fond memories here. You know, it was a simpler time back then, and I thought the place deserved to be restored to its former glory."

She's interested in that, so I take her around the camp, showing her what Grant and I have been up to, the contrast between the things we've fixed and the things we haven't. And as predicted, it's not long before we're by the lake and Samilla grins, sucking in a deep breath, the sun in her face.

"Well, I can certainly see the appeal of leaving the city behind with a view like this!"

"I eat lunch every day at that picnic table over there. Couldn't ask for a better spot."

"Why don't we go take a seat and talk some more?"

I nod and follow her over to the table. Howard's following too, but he's constantly moving, getting different shots and angles. I try to just ignore him like she told me to, to pretend he's not there.

Samilla sits down opposite me and folds her hands, looking rather serious. "I know we've had fun today touring the camp, but the reason we're here isn't fun at all."

"No, it isn't," I agree.

"Let's talk about Jack and his accusations. Is that okay?"

"Sure," I say, acid rising in my chest, burning and churning, but I swallow it down. I haven't done anything wrong. The only grievance anyone on that team had with me was my sexuality.

"What's your impression of Jack Alsworth?"

I sigh, shaking my head. "To be honest, I never really had much of one. He joined the team and I think they had him on the roster as someone to train up in a couple years, you know? But he never really worked for the team and only lasted a season. I never spent any time with him outside of practice and games."

"So you never came on to him?"

I shake my head again. "Definitely not. While I was still in the league, I did everything I could to keep my sexuality under wraps. Coming on to a teammate would have torched all that hard work."

Samilla frowns. "Can I ask why you chose to live in

secret?"

"It's complicated, really. You've seen how people react to just the *rumor* I might be gay… And then as soon as I confirm it, someone's accusing me of being a predator. It's not a very friendly climate to be out and proud in the sports world right now."

"You don't think your teammates would have supported you?"

I actually clench my jaw at that, my knuckles tightening on the edge of the table. "That's what gets me the most about all of this, to be honest. When I *was* outed, there was no support. I was shunned and bullied and basically pushed out of the team. Even the people I thought were my friends turned their backs on me. So the idea that there's some *conspiracy* to cover up me hitting on Jack is just laughable. They were not on my side *at all* when they found out."

Samilla's eyebrows are high on her forehead, her mouth slightly parted. "I had no idea you were so mistreated."

I shrug. "It's not something I dwell on or want to make a big deal out of; it's just the way things happened. My team-mates found out I'm gay and made me feel so unwelcome that I ended up retiring from the game. It's not some big cover-up of anything other than me just trying to stay in the closet. But I'm done with that now. I'm not ashamed of who I am, and I'm not going to let someone use my vulnerability for their own gain."

I hate talking about it like this. I hate being so open, but I know it's necessary. If people are going to hear my side of things, they need to hear my *whole* side. Even if it means throwing some people I was close to under the bus. They certainly didn't stick their necks out for me. Right now, the most important thing is getting my story out there and making sure Grant and I can have a future together.

There are a few more follow-up questions, but for the

most part, the interview is over. Finally, Samilla gestures at Howard again and he lowers the camera.

Samilla grins at me from ear to ear. "That was *amazing!* I'm so glad you decided to share your side of the story. There's so much that hasn't been put out there yet."

"I hope you've got something useful," I grumble, not sure anymore if this was such a good idea. I know how journalists are, and I know how deceptive video editing can be. They could use the footage from today and take everything I said out of context and make me look even guiltier than before.

Of course they *can* do that. I just have to trust that they won't. I have to trust that they're operating in good faith, and I can't dwell on the worst possible outcome. Not when there are already enough things stacked against me. At this point, I have to be optimistic or there's no room left for hope.

"Oh, absolutely. I'm going to talk to my producer and see if we can't get this aired ASAP. I'd love to sit around and chat some more, but if we want to make it on the air tomorrow, we need to get this footage edited today."

"Tomorrow?" I squeak, surprised by the sound of my own voice coming out so startled.

"Hopefully!" she says, holding up crossed fingers.

Before they leave, I get Howard to scribble down his address, promising to send Joey an autographed ball as soon as I can. Samilla's not in any mood to wait around now that she's got what she wants.

As they leave, Grant comes over, looking at me expectantly.

"Well? How'd it go?"

I bite my lip, my hands in my pockets. "Okay, I think?"

"You think?"

"It happened kind of fast. You sure this reporter is okay?"

He nods. "As sure as I can be. What did she say? Are they going to print your story?"

"She's hoping to have it on the air *tomorrow*," I say, still having trouble believing the reality of that.

"You're kidding!"

"No?"

"That's amazing! You should call Mila and let her know."

"Do you think I should have talked to my lawyer before going to the press?" I ask, suddenly feeling like an idiot for not thinking of that sooner.

Grant also looks like the conflict only just occurred to him. "A little late now, isn't it?"

I sigh. "Guess so."

"It'll be fine," he says, sliding his arm around my waist.

"I hope so."

He kisses the side of my neck, then the scratchy edge of my jaw. His lips capture mine and everything else fades into the background. Everything in this moment is just Grant.

"I think there's probably work to do," I say as his hand snakes down my front to cup my growing erection.

"I think there's been enough work done today," he says, his fingers stroking me, making me suck in a sharp breath.

"You think so, huh?"

He nods, kissing me again. "I do. You've had a hard day. I think you could use some comforting."

"Is that so?" I ask, smirking, grinding forward into him, watching his eyelids flutter shut for just a moment as he sighs. I swear, with Grant the anticipation is nearly as good as the actual thing.

"Do you disagree?"

I bite his bottom lip and his moan sends a surge of heat straight to my balls. "Not even a little."

GRANT

$\mathcal{W}$aking up in bed next to Ian is maybe the best thing that's ever happened to me. Other than Ian himself, of course.

He's radiating warmth and his strong arms are wrapped around me. I can feel his heart beating in his chest, and even though he's still snoring softly, there's one part of him that's already awake. And as tempting as it is, I extract myself from his embrace, kissing him softly as I climb out of the bed.

I know he's trying to play it cool, he's trying to act like it doesn't matter that much, but his interview is supposed to be airing today, and I want to do everything I can to have him relaxed when it comes out.

Besides, keeping busy keeps my mind from dwelling on it. I am my mother's son after all, so taking care of people is how I deal with being stressed. So I head into the kitchen and start raiding his fridge, scrounging up what I can for breakfast. There's a carton of eggs, cheese, some milk and a few veggies laying around. Perfect for a frittata. Can't go wrong with what's essentially a giant omelet, right?

I just hope I didn't make a mistake convincing Ian to talk

to Samilla. I hope that she's a genuine as she seemed. I hope that she didn't trick us into giving her all the ammo she needs to make Ian a villain.

I'll never forgive myself if that's the case. I talked him into inviting her out. If she drags him through the mud, it's all my fault. If this makes things worse… I'll just feel awful.

I know Ian wouldn't blame me, but the guilt would kill me. I try not to think about it while I'm making breakfast and cleaning up around the cabin. Not that there's much to clean up. Ian hardly spends any time inside unless we're in here together, and then we're not exactly using the rooms other than the bedroom…

I'm cleaning the windows when he comes stumbling out in his full naked glory, scratching the back of his head and wincing at the daylight.

"Something smells amazing."

"Breakfast," I answer, not leaving the window until this stubborn spot comes off.

"Wow, I get breakfast?" He comes up behind me, wraps his arms around my waist, and I feel his hardness pressing into the cleft of my ass. I lean back into him despite myself, and shiver.

"I thought it would be nice."

"It is," he says, kissing me gently, slowly enough to make my head spin.

"Is it ready?" he asks, kissing up the side of my neck, his hands sliding down my front.

"In about two minutes," I answer, trying to resist the heat he's stoking to life within me.

"Darn."

"You're not looking forward to my breakfast?" I fake-pout.

"You better believe I am."

I turn back to the window, that spot still there, and Ian

leans forward.

"What?" I ask.

"Just wondering what's got you so serious."

"There's a spot," I grumble, scraping at it with my nail.

"Uh-huh. It's a cabin in the woods, Grant. It's dirty."

"It doesn't *have* to be—" He wraps his fingers around my wrist and pulls my hand away from the window.

"What's going on?"

I frown. "Who says anything's going on?"

"You made breakfast and you're cleaning instead of being in bed with me."

"Like that's so unthinkable?"

He grins, pulling me tighter against him. My traitorous body melts and I sigh. "Yes."

"There's that ego again," I mutter, but there's no bite to it. My voice is airy and light while he's got me in his arms.

He's still got my wrist and he pulls my hand back, resting it on his naked cock. "That's not an ego," he says.

I sigh, stroking him, and then the timer for the frittata goes off.

Ian growls, but lets me go fetch breakfast from the oven. By the time I've got it out and delivered to the table, he's found a pair of sweatpants and put them on. Unfortunately.

At least now he can't distract me.

"Don't think you're getting out of our discussion so easily," he says, pointing a fork at me once we've both made a plate.

"Our discussion?" I ask innocently.

"Something's on your mind. I can tell."

"Has anyone ever told you you're annoyingly persistent?"

"I've heard something like that before, yes."

I roll my eyes and huff. "I'm just worried about this interview thing. I don't know how it's going to turn out and I'm worried for you. For us."

Ian's cavalier grin drops and he reaches across the table to take my hand, his face serious. "It's going to be fine. No matter how it turns out, I don't care about what the world thinks. All I care about is that I have you with me."

I smile at him across the table, my heart swelling with emotion. How did I get so lucky? How does a man like Ian want me?

From the bedroom, his cell rings. I can tell he's going to ignore it, so I pull my hand back.

"Answer it. It might be Perry."

Ian sighs, rolling his eyes, but he knows I'm right and he leaves to get the phone. I hear the ringing stop before he gets to it though.

"Who was it?"

"Samilla," he answers, sitting back down. A second later, the phone chimes again. Ian looks at the screen, his brow furrowing.

"What?"

"They're airing the piece at eleven."

"A.M.?"

He nods.

My eyes dart to the clock on the microwave. "That's only an hour from now."

"Yep," he says, much less worried about all of this than I am. He takes a bite of the frittata and gives me a thumbs up.

"This is great. One of your mom's recipes?"

I'm kind of stunned by how he's just brushing this whole thing off and doesn't seem concerned about it at all, but I try to adopt the same attitude. "No, one of mine, actually. Eggs are cheap when you're a broke college kid."

And like that, we get through breakfast with weird generic conversation that completely ignores all the stuff happening around us. I'm watching the clock constantly as we clear the table together, wash the dishes, put them away.

Finally, it gets to a quarter to the hour and I can't take it anymore.

"Aren't we going to watch the interview?" I burst.

Ian frowns. "I'm not sure I want to…"

"Don't you want to see how it turned out?"

He sighs. "I guess I should. Seems weird to watch myself on TV."

"Come on," I say, taking him by the hand, leading him to the couch. "We'll watch it together. What's the point of having satellite out here if you can't watch yourself on TV?"

"I don't think that's most people's reasoning," he teases,sitting down next to me, his arm around my shoulders. I snuggle into his chest, turning the TV on to the right channel.

"If this interview makes me a monster, you're not going to leave me, right?" he asks, and I hear that he's trying to inject some humor into his tone, but I also hear the worry in it. I can tell there's some truth to those fears.

I take his hand in mine, lacing our fingers together, and sit up straighter so I can look him in the eyes. "I'm not going anywhere," I say. Then, I take a deep breath. Now is the time. I know it is. I know it's been coming for a while and I've been waiting for the moment. Now that it's here I don't know how I'll actually manage to say it. I'm just going to have to spit it out all at once. "I'll always be with you. I love you and I'll be at your side for as long as you want me."

He looks at me for a long moment and I think I just screwed everything up. Maybe it wasn't the right time. Maybe it's still too soon. Maybe he thinks I'm crazy.

He kisses me, long and slow, our lips melding until I'm not sure where I end and he starts. It's delicious and indulgent and I never want it to end. But when it does, he says the sweetest words I've ever heard.

"I love you too." His hand cups my jaw, his one good

thumb stroking my cheek, our eyes locked together, lost in each other. Neither one of us needs to say anything else, because it's all right there in our eyes.

I'm so wrapped up in Ian and our confessions of love that I forget why we're on the couch in front of the TV until I hear his voice. It startles Ian more than me and we both laugh nervously.

"It's always weird hearing my own voice," he says.

"But look how cute you are on screen," I offer, grinning wide.

He rolls his eyes. "You'd say that even if I looked terrible."

"You're wrong. You could never look terrible."

He laughs and shakes his head, pulling me tight against him as we watch Samilla's story with rapt attention.

It's weird to see the camp on TV, to see the place where we had our first kiss, to watch Ian pour his heart out to someone who's basically a stranger. But I'm proud of him for doing it. He shows some real raw, honest emotion, and at least in my opinion, he comes off as very sympathetic.

Samilla transitions from her interview with Ian to clips of her talking to his former teammates. I feel him instantly tense next to me and I know he's preparing himself for his former friends to throw him under the bus.

"How did you react when you found out Ian was gay?" Samilla asks, a microphone in a guy's face. He looks guilty, unable to meet the camera with his eyes.

"You know… I wish I could say I handled it better, but I didn't. We didn't do right by Ian and I know I'm not the only one who regrets it. A lot of the guys feel real bad about how it all went down, especially with all this stuff with Jack happening."

And that guy's not the only one. Samilla talks to a couple other guys that say the same thing, corroborating Ian's side of things. She also talks to a couple of guys that are suspiciously quiet on the subject. The same guys that were labeled as the worst of the bullies.

"And what does Coach Montez have to say about Jack?" on-screen Samilla says. The video cuts to a stern-looking older man behind a desk, surrounded by memorabilia.

"Jack's public announcement is the first I'd heard of any *allegations*. He consistently failed routine drug tests and the Hawks decided to terminate their relationship with Mr. Alsworth. The decision had nothing to do with any other player."

There are a few more clips with Samilla driving the points home, but that seems like a freaking home run to me. I heave a sigh of relief and turn to Ian, who's just staring at the TV in shock.

"Is it just me, or did that actually go really well?" he asks.

I laugh and hug him tight. "It was amazing! You did so well and Jack's lost all credibility. I don't know how he could go forward with the suit at this point."

Ian grins, hugging me back. "We can't get our hopes up yet until it's all official with the lawyers."

"Look who's going by the books now," I tease.

He smirks. "No one can be a reckless rebel with a bad boy attitude all the time."

I snort. "Were you ever that?"

"Hey, you didn't know me before. I was a player," he protests.

"Before what?" I ask, happiness threatening to bubble over. I knew I was worried about the interview, but I guess I didn't realize *how* worried until it was all over and everything was okay.

"Before I fell in love and realized that life wasn't for me anymore."

...How could I *not* fall for that?

IAN

*G*rant spent the night again. I tried to tell him that his mom's going to get annoyed with *me* if he doesn't cut it out, but there's no talking him out of it. And I'm not really trying all that hard anyway. I like having him in my bed. I like having him in my arms. I don't want it to change, but there's still so much up in the air that I'm not sure how I'm going to avoid that happening.

I'm just lying in bed holding him when my phone rings. He mutters in his sleep, but I kiss his temple and shush him, slipping out with my phone.

"Perry?" I answer, closing the bedroom door behind me.

"Ian, hope I didn't wake you?"

"No, what's up?"

"Is there any way you could come in to the office today? There have been... developments."

I look back at the door. I know behind it Grant's sleeping, sleeping and not worrying. I don't want to exclude him, but I *do* want to protect him.

"Is it something I need to be there in person for?" I ask. "It's a three-hour drive."

"You're going to have to be here in person to sign any documentation—"

"Why don't you tell me what the documentation is, and then I'll decide if it's worth driving three hours both ways to sign."

Perry sighs and I almost feel bad. He is Mila's husband after all. I don't want to annoy her or burn any bridges there, but I am still paying him his going rate, so I expect certain things from my lawyers. Mainly not wasting my time.

"Jack has offered to sign an NDA in exchange for a small settlement. This whole thing can be taken care of out of court before the day's over if you want."

"A settlement?"

"No-fault," Perry adds quickly. "You're not admitting guilt in any way; it's just get him to drop the suit."

"So it's extortion," I grumble.

Perry sighs again and I can just imagine the poor guy going grayer by the minute.

"I know it's not exactly what you wanted, but you did tell me you want this over quickly. Guys like Jack… all they care about is getting a payday. If you want my advice, take the deal and move on with your life."

It is tempting. I do want this all over. I want it behind me so I can forget about it and not be constantly reminded by this sword that's hanging over my head.

But I think about how Grant would react to me taking the settlement deal. I remember how much he wants me to fight these allegations and clear my name.

And with Samilla's interview out there, I think my chances are better than ever. Like I told her, I'm not going to roll over and let him take advantage of me.

"No deal," I say.

"Ian—"

"No deal. I have a counteroffer for him: withdraw the

lawsuit and issue a public apology or I'll sue *him* for everything he's worth."

"That's not even enough to cover my fees," Perry mumbles.

"I don't care. It's not about the money. I just want him to admit the truth. To admit that he's a homophobic liar in front of the whole world."

"Yeah, all right," Perry says, exasperated, but resigned. "I'll draft the letter and call you when I've got anything to tell you."

"Great. Thanks a ton."

He ends the call without any more pleasantries and I know he's annoyed with me, but he's my lawyer. He doesn't have to like me. Jack Alsworth went after the wrong guy.

If it weren't for Grant, I might just lie down and let him walk all over me, but I'm not that guy anymore. I'm not going to be ashamed for being who I am. I'm not going to let someone mistreat me and rationalize it as me deserving it or something like that. It's bullshit and it ends now.

The door behind me opens and Grant's there, rubbing his eyes sleepily. He looks so damn cute I just want to kiss him senseless and drag him back to bed.

"Were you on the phone?" he asks, blinking away sleep.

"Yeah."

He tilts his head to the side in a question and I know I can't lie to him or try to play it off.

"It was Perry. Jack wants to settle."

In a split second Grant's face changes, his eyes harden, his jaw clenches. "What?"

"Yeah, he agreed to sign an NDA for a small settlement and Perry told me I should take it."

"So were you just making a decision without me?" he asks, folding his arms.

"I was trying to protect you, so I handled it."

"Protect me? Do you realize how ridiculous that sounds? We're supposed to be in this together, Ian. You can't protect me from decisions that affect us both."

"You're right," I say quickly. "I wasn't trying to start a fight or anything, Grant, I swear."

He huffs, but drops his arms to his side, letting me grab him by the hips and pull him into me.

"Did you settle?" he finally asks, like he's worried the words are going to prompt a scorpion to sting him.

"No. I wouldn't do that to us. You made it clear to me how you feel about that."

He sighs and looks somewhat appeased. "Fine. Good. But if we are in a relationship, we have to share the big decisions."

"You're absolutely right," I agree. "This whole relationship thing is as new for me as it is for you, you know."

He grins. "I *like* this 'whole relationship thing,'" he says.

"Me too." I pause for a long moment, frowning. "You sure you want to fight this thing out with Jack? It could get ugly. They might come after your family. Especially with how close we were growing up. They could try to twist our relationship…"

"Ian, nothing's going to convince me to not be with you, and definitely not some hackneyed reporters for sports magazines I don't even read."

"This is serious."

"I'm being serious," he says, kissing me, smiling. "I think we have a dock to finish."

I grin. I don't know what I did to deserve an amazing man like Grant, but boy am I glad it happened. "I think you're right."

And for the rest of the day, we forget the outside world with its scandals and lawsuits and judgments. We forget about everything but our work and each other, and when we're all sweaty from building up the dock, we strip down and swim together in the lake, making out on the shore as the sun dries us and warms us up again.

It's a perfect day.

GRANT

J swear this dock is never going to be done. Every time it seems like we're almost through with it, we find some other problem that needs to be addressed. Ian's spending a ton of time in the water, making sure everything's as stable as it can be. He's really focused on safety, which I appreciate, but I also want to be done with this part of the job.

Every time he disappears under the water, I have to hold my breath with him, pushing back the fears that he's not coming back up.

Even though he's taught me to swim and I'm a lot more comfortable in the water than I was at the beginning of this summer, I still don't like it. I don't like being near the water. I still feel like it's trying to draw me in, pull me under, trap me where I can't escape.

I still get nervous shakes whenever the water is higher than my waist. Unless Ian's holding my hand, of course.

It's been a few days since Jack tried to get Ian to settle, and we haven't heard anything from Perry or Mila about the case. So when Ian's phone rings from the shore, I jump and squint at it, like I'll somehow be able to figure out who it is calling just by staring at it from a hundred feet away.

Obviously, I don't have that superpower, so I have no idea who's calling. But the phone's ringing and Ian's under water where he can't hear it. I lean over the dock's edge and dip my hand into the water, waving it around to try to get his attention. But he's either too busy with what he's doing or the water's too murky to see, because he doesn't seem to notice.

The ringing stops and I curse, hoping we didn't just miss an important call, but it rings again almost immediately and now I know it's *got* to be Perry. Who else would be this persistent?

There's no way I'm answering Ian's phone for him though, that's a line I wouldn't cross. Thankfully, just as I'm thinking about diving in after him—he has been under for a long time, but he's been getting a lot of practice with this lately—his head surfaces and he sucks in deep gulping breaths.

"Your phone's ringing," I say quickly as he frowns at the strange sound. "You just missed a call and they're calling right back."

Ian's eyes go wide and he makes the same connection I do. "Perry," he says it like it's a curse under his breath and then starts to pull himself up on the dock.

Even now, I can't help but watch the way his muscles flex, dripping in the afternoon sun. I lick my lips and shake my head, trying to focus as he stumbles up to shore and snatches his phone up just as it stops ringing.

"Was it him?" I call up the hill.

"Yeah, I'm going to call him back."

While Ian's making the call, I head up to him, lingering nearby to hear what I can. I'm not going to let him leave me out of this again.

"Okay... No. Absolutely not. He knows the terms, I'm not renegotiating again," Ian says, hanging up the phone.

I raise my eyebrows at him in a question and he scrubs his hand over his head, blowing out a breath.

"Jack wants to drop the whole thing without the public apology," he says. Instantly, my whole body goes rigid. I'm seeing red, and my blood goes hot.

"Easy, you heard me. I told him no," Ian says, squeezing my shoulder.

"Yeah, I know. It just makes me so angry that he thinks he can make this up, rip apart your life, and then get out of it without admitting any wrongdoing."

He shrugs. "Some people never want to take responsibility for their actions. It's more common than you'd think in professional sports. These are the guys that got away with murder in school because they brought in money for their programs and communities. You grow up having people clean up your messes for you and then you suddenly don't know how to hold a broom."

"You're being really understanding about all of this," I say, still pouting about it. I hate Jack Alsworth for what he's put Ian through. I don't think he deserves any leniency or forgiveness.

Ian smiles and slides his hand up to cup the side of my face. "I love that you want to protect me and right all the wrongs, but I'm not going to let him ruin the happiness I've found with you."

"You big sap," I tease, kissing him, smiling despite myself.

He grins back. "Only with you."

"I think I'm okay with that."

"I've just about got the supports fully secured down there. One more trip underwater and I should be good."

"You better be," I say, frowning. "I hate watching you go down there."

"So I shouldn't tell you that I'm considering a new career in scuba diving?"

I give him a look and he laughs, holding up his hands. "Kidding, kidding. I promise."

Before we even get to the dock, his phone's ringing again. We both look at it expectantly.

"Guess Jack's done dragging this out," Ian says, jogging back to his phone with a grin.

But when he picks it up off the picnic table, he frowns at it, then answers.

"Hello?"

So it isn't Perry then. I frown and head back to him, hoping to pick up on some of the conversation.

But there's not much to pick up on, because Ian's just listening quietly, his face unreadable. I don't know if it's good news or bad news or something in between because he's giving me nothing.

"Okay, thanks for calling. I'll have to think about it."

I'm looking at him expectantly as he hangs up the call, but Ian looks past me, out over to the lake, his eyes distant and vacant.

"Ian?"

"Hmm?"

"Who was it?" I prompt.

"Samilla," he says, sounding as distant as his gaze looks. He seems distracted. What the hell could that call have been about?

"What did she say? Do they want another interview?"

"No," he says. "They want to offer me a job."

"What?!" The moment he says it, I'm excited, but he doesn't sound excited. He sounds like he's not sure he's even going to accept it, so I temper my enthusiasm. It's not easy. "What do you mean?"

"The network liked my interview," he says, everything

monotone, like he's reciting something from a script. "They liked my camera presence, and when the whole Jack thing dies down, they'd like me to be a regular."

"That's amazing! You'd be working from the station in the city where my job will be... We'll still be close enough for weekend trips to Umberland. It's perfect!"

But as excited as I am, Ian isn't. He doesn't look like he thinks this is perfect at all.

"It's definitely something to think about," he says, scratching his chin thoughtfully. "But it would mean not restoring the camp, giving up on that dream..."

All at once, I deflate. Of course he has dreams too. I was being so selfish thinking this was the answer to all our problems. But I know I want to be with Ian, no matter the sacrifice. I know I want him in my life.

"Well, I could always stay here with you instead of taking the job in the city. You mean more to me than any job," I say, clinging to him. And it's true. He does. He's everything to me, but it would hurt to not take that opportunity when it's such a big deal. Getting a job offer after the first interview for a job that's way above where I hoped to start seems too good to pass up.

But it's still nothing compared to being with Ian.

Ian shakes his head. "I need time to think," he says, his face serious and closed off. "We'll talk about it later."

I frown. "Okay, but... I thought we agreed you weren't going to keep me out of the decision-making processes anymore?"

He sighs and grabs my hips, squeezing. "I know." He's quiet for a long moment, his head hung low, his shoulders slumped.

"I'm sorry," he finally says, his voice strained. "I'm not trying to cut you out. I just... I want to walk through the camp and figure out what's important. What I need to do, you know?"

I bite my bottom lip. I do understand where he's coming from. We both have a lot invested in this decision emotionally and it could get ugly if we were to try to hash it out together before he knows what he really wants.

I kiss him softly and meet his eyes. "You do what you have to do, and then you come back to me, okay?"

He nods. "I promise."

And with that, I back off. I head up to the main cabin, sure I can find something to work on up there while Ian sorts out his thoughts. I just hope he doesn't take too long because the not knowing is going to kill me.

IAN

A job at ESPN?

That's crazy.

That's bigger than crazy. I don't even know what it is.

But it's also a job back in the city. It's leaving Umberland again, leaving this camp that Grant and I have put so much work into.

My mind's racing a million miles a second and it's all I can do not to tear my own hair out. But walking helps. The fresh air helps. The big pines and oaks crushing in, blotting out the sunlight help.

Instead of focusing on all those things I don't know the answer to, I try to slow down, take a deep breath, close my eyes, and listen to the sounds of the forest. The chattering of squirrels, the whisper of bird wings high above the trees.

It's calming. It's peaceful. But then I open my eyes and look around me. I'm beyond the front few cabins we've been working on and it's even worse than I remember. There's a building that used to be a cafeteria, but now the roof's caved in. That's not something I'm going to be able to fix alone. There are more cabins back here, but they're even more overgrown, lost to the woods. The place where there used to be a dance hall for those special occasions in Umberland is nothing but rubble. It's going to have to be rebuilt from the ground up.

I don't know what I was thinking when I bought this place.

There's no way I'll be able to have it up and running by next summer. I don't know if I really want to spend another whole year rebuilding everything without any payoff.

All the old paths out here are overgrown and hard to make out, but there's one path I don't need any help finding. I remember the three-trunk oak, and even though the way is nothing but brush and vines now, I make my way down around it. I go past a thicket of blackberry, down to the water where a bunch of us used to launch off of an unsanctioned rope swing.

After all these years, there's not much left of the old rope, but it's still there, the branch it's tied around starting to grow up over it. I scramble up onto the rock we used to jump off of and just look out over the glittering surface of the water. I pick up a handful of rocks, and consider each one before deciding whether to drop it or skip it. Watching the rocks skim across the water has always helped me think. It helps me get my thoughts in order. So the whole time I'm going through everything in my head, I'm just standing on the rock, skipping stones, watching them sail off before finally disappearing into the depths.

There are so many memories here. Memories of a happier time. An easier time, when there wasn't any controversy over my love life. As much as I loved those days and sometimes long for the simplicity of it all, I wouldn't go back to it. Not now. Now that I've got Grant.

He asked me once why I decided to buy this camp, and I gave some bullshit answer about how I wanted to help other people make great memories. But all I'm really doing here is hiding in my own. Things exploded in my life, and I ran back home and hid. I tried to relive my childhood by buying the old camp, and none of that was ever going to make it any better. I'd be lying to myself if I thought it was.

I can't just stay hidden here because I have fond memories. I can't just cling to the past at the cost of Grant's happiness.

Besides, Grant's inspired a change in me. Even I'm not blind enough to miss it. For the first time in my life, I'm not afraid to kiss the person I'm with in public. Or hold their hand. I'm not ashamed to love Grant, and I don't care if the whole damn world knows it. I *want* them to know it.

I can't let him give up his dreams for me. Just the thought of him doing that hurts. He's worked so hard to get as far as he has and I'm not going to let him throw it all away for me because I'm having some kind of crisis and can't face the real world.

No way.

Grant needs me to suck it up and be there for him. Be supportive for him. Grant needs a guy that isn't afraid to stand up for what's right even when it's hard. If it had just been me when Jack made his claims, I probably would have settled to not have to deal with it. Because that's the easy way out. Just like running back to Umberland to hide was the easy way out.

But Grant's taught me that doing what's right isn't always easy. Standing up to Jack is proving to be a pain in the ass every step of the way, but I know that Grant's right. We can't let him get away with this. Not just for me, not just for us, but for all the people that are stereotyped based on their sexuality.

Standing up to Jack isn't easy, and going back to the city won't be easy either. But it's what's right. Moving to the city to be with Grant, to take this job—I know it's the right thing. Being on a major network as a representative of a group that wouldn't normally get representation in my field… It's an important cause, and there are times it might be difficult.

But it's the right thing to do. So I know I'm going to do it.

I skip the last stone, watch it hop along, before finally sinking. I watch the water until the ripples it created have all faded into the lake's waves, and then I turn away, making my way back up the path to the three-trunked oak.

Now that I know I'm leaving, this camp looks in even worse shape. I know it's fixable, and I know someone with better resources than me will be able to restore it to its former glory, but right now… This part of the woods might as well be condemned.

At least the front portion is looking good. That's something. Maybe the next owner can rent out the cabins to help fund further renovations. It's an idea, but not one I'm going to pursue.

I find Grant putting together the second picnic table that we'd already cut the boards for. Most guys would have just left for their own "time to think" after all of that, but not Grant. Grant's still hard at work. Because that's just the kind of guy he is. That's just the kind of guy *my* guy is.

He looks up as my shadow falls over him and I can tell he doesn't know what to think. He's not sure if he should smile or frown or look concerned, and it's all adorable because I know he's just trying for me. I grab him by the wrist and pull him up to me, kissing him deep, his lips salty from sweat.

"Well, hi to you too," he says, breathless as I pull back.

"I'm going to take the job," I blurt out. "We can come home on weekends whenever you want. Or not, as the case may be."

He grins at me, his fingers tickling the hair at the nape of my neck. "What are you going to do with the camp?"

I shrug. "Find someone better than me to take care of it. Someone that isn't just looking for a project to distract them from their problems."

"Is that what happened here?" he asks. "What changed?"

"Someone came and made all my problems go away," I say, nipping at his neck.

"I don't think that's very accurate," he says, squirming. "I'm pretty sure you still have problems."

I shrug again. "If I've got you, they're nothing."

"You sure?"

I arch a brow at him. "Did you have something particular in mind?" I know that smirky scheming look. He doesn't get it often, but when Grant's feeling playful, there's no mistaking it.

"I was thinking we could go break the terrible news to my mother."

"You just want a buffer," I mumble in between kisses along his collarbone.

"You're right. But that's what boyfriends are for, isn't it?"

"Is that all?"

He grins. "Oh no, I've got a whole list."

I can't help grinning back. "What have I gotten myself into?"

"You're dating a Rainier; nothing good."

I groan and roll my eyes exaggeratedly, but I couldn't be happier. Grant is everything I ever wanted and didn't think I'd ever deserve. But somehow, he came into my life and flipped it upside down and made me a better, stronger man for it. A man full of joy and optimism and love instead of cynicism and suspicion.

I take him by the hand and lead him down toward my truck. We hold hands the whole drive to his parents' house and it's not until the house is actually in sight that I realize what's happening.

I've been to the Rainier house a billion times. And I've even seen Sheryl and Trevor out and about since Grant and I have become "official," but I haven't been to the house since then. And now I'm coming into their house to tell them that I'm moving with their baby boy to the city, far away where they can't protect him.

Grant walks right in, dragging me behind him. Reflexively, I want to let go of his hand, but he's holding on tight, and I'm grateful for it. I'm done hiding how I feel. From anyone.

"Hello?" Grant calls.

"In here, cupcake!" Sheryl answers from the kitchen. Unsurprisingly. Also unsurprisingly, she's making cupcakes.

"Smells good," I say, taking a deep breath.

"You've gotta wait at least half an hour," she answers, waggling her finger at me. Then she notices us holding hands, notices Grant grinning so hard he's about to break his jaw, and she narrows her eyes.

"What is it?"

"Ian got a job offer in the city too!"

Her eyes go wide, she looks at me for a minute and I actually want to shrink away and hide from it. But then her look softens and she sighs, shaking her head. "I wish it weren't so far, but I'm happy for you, baby. You too, Ian," she says, hugging us each in turn. She quickly turns back to mixing up her buttercream, but I'm sure I see something sparkle in her eye, a tear maybe.

"Greg, Scout, get in here!"

"Oh you don't have to—"

Grant squeezes my hand, cutting me off, leaning in to whisper, "Just let it happen. You're *really* a part of the family now, so there's no escaping this stuff."

I squeeze his hand back. I'm pretty sure I'm perfectly okay with that.

"If you're testing another one of those B.S. sugar-free recipes, I don't want any part of it," Greg grumbles as he shuffles into the kitchen.

"I'm not, and keep your greasy paws off my cupcakes until they're cool," Sheryl says, swatting at him with a kitchen towel.

I hear Scout coming down soon after, and it's almost just like the old days. But better. Definitely better.

"You should call Trevor and tell him too," she says, waving at Grant. He nods, chuckling.

"Tell him what?" asks Scout from the doorway.

"We're moving to the city together. Ian got a job offer at ESPN."

Scout's eyes go wide and she sinks into a chair. "Are you serious? You're going to be on TV?!"

"Uh… Yeah, I guess I am," I say, chuckling awkwardly. I guess I hadn't really thought about *that* part of the job, but I'm used to being on camera. I've given a million interviews. It'll definitely be weird to be on the other side of it though. But it's kind of exciting now that I'm thinking about it. It's a new challenge. Something I never even really considered, but now it's fallen in my lap, it kind of makes perfect sense.

It's only about ten minutes before Sheryl cracks and ices her too-warm cupcakes for us to eat in celebration. She's still a little choked up over Grant leaving, but I can tell she's also happy for us.

"I've got to be honest, I was worried you guys wouldn't take us being together nearly this well," I say, licking a dab of frosting from my thumb.

Greg and Sheryl exchange a look. The kind of look that only comes with nearly forty years of marriage.

"It was never going to be easy for us to accept anyone that Grant brought home," Sheryl says. "He's our baby—"

"*Mom*—"

"It's *true*. Maybe you'll understand one day if you have kids of your own, but the baby has a special place in your heart."

"Gee thanks, Mom," Scout mutters, smirking.

Sheryl ignores her for the most part, only sending her a look. "The point is, you've always been there for Trevor, and we know that you'll take good care of Grant. There's no one we'd rather see him end up with."

There's a sudden lump in my throat and I swallow it, blinking quickly, nodding, hoping the combination of all of that can hide how touched I am. "That means a lot," I finally choke out.

Grant squeezes my hand and I've never felt so at home in all my life as I do here with the Rainiers. With Grant.

"Trevor says congratulations," Grant says, tucking his phone quickly in his pocket. I'm pretty sure that's not at all what Trevor actually said, and that just makes me smile harder. Prickly bastard. I know he's happy for us too.

IAN

*N*ow that I've made the decision to leave Umberland and go back to the city, there's so much that needs to get done. I need to pack—not that I ever did much in the way of *un*packing—and I need to make this place more attractive to a buyer. Not that I need to sell it right away. I can wait for the right person to come around, and in the meantime, I can host all the Rainiers here for cookouts and swimming. There are still a couple of weeks of summer left. We could still have some fun before the camp is out of my hands.

I guess Grant has been kind of living in limbo the past few weeks, not knowing if he's going to accept the job or not... because of me. So now that I've stopped dragging my feet and made up my mind, he's got a lot of packing and arrangements to make too. We're going to be looking at apartments soon, but right now, we're just making our own individual preparations. Doing this without him makes me miss him a little.

My phone rings sometime around noon and I jump at it, hoping that it's Grant wanting to grab lunch in town, but it's

Perry on the caller ID.

"Perry, tell me you've got good news," I say, answering with my heart in my throat.

"Hope you don't have dinner plans tonight, kid. Jack's apology is happening live tonight at six o'clock, so make sure you tune in."

"Really? He's doing it?" I can't believe it. I didn't really think Jack was ever going to swallow his pride enough to make a public apology, but the fact that he is just proves that much more how right Grant was about the whole thing.

"He is."

"All right. Go ahead and drop the countersuit once he's dropped his."

"His lawyer had the dismissal notice sent my way this morning. He's already dropped it. It's over; you won. That interview you did really had him by the balls."

I grin. "That reminds me, I need to talk to your wife about the latest job offer I got. Seems I might be needing an agent again after all."

"I'm glad the son of a bitch didn't get what he wanted."

"Me too. I can't thank you enough."

Perry chuckles. "The trip to Turks and Caicos that you're funding is all the thanks I need."

"Glad to hear it."

After I end the call with Perry, I call Grant right away, bursting at the seams to share the good news with him.

"Jack's apologizing on air today," I blurt out as soon as he answers, not even able to play it cool. I didn't realize how much this whole thing really was weighing on me until now. I tried to play it cool. Tried to seem like I wasn't worried. But how could I not be?

"He's what?"

"You heard me," I say, grinning. "Perry just called to say he's accepted my terms. He's dropped the suit and he's going on live TV tonight to apologize for putting me through all this."

"You did it! I knew you could do it. I'm so proud of you, babe!" The pet name just makes me smile more. I never thought I'd be into something like that, but with Grant, everything's different. I'm different. And I love it.

"When is it airing? I want to be there to watch it with you."

"Six."

"I'll bring pizza and beer to celebrate."

"I love you."

He laughs. "You're too easy."

"Not because of the beer and pizza," I say, knowing he's just teasing me, having fun teasing him back. There's nothing better than this. Than the two of us together, even just on the phone.

"I love you because none of this amazing stuff would have happened without you."

"You're pretty amazing yourself, you know," he says, and I can hear him smiling through the phone.

"How's the packing coming along?"

"I keep getting distracted," he sighs. "Remind me never to look through my old yearbooks ever again."

That makes me laugh. "Oh no, you're going to have to show me those later."

"Not a chance!"

"We'll see about that," I growl, and I hear the little hitch in his voice, the sound he makes when I turn him on. I love that sound. I love knowing what it means, what I'm doing to him.

"So I'll see you at six?"

"It's a date," he says, quickly adding, "Love you."

"I love you too," I say, hanging up the phone with my heart still beating so fast I feel like it's going to beat right through my chest. Saying that out loud is still hard for me;

it's strange and unusual, but I *like* it. I like that Grant's the only guy I've ever said that to. I like that when I say it to him, I mean it without a doubt.

I figure I might as well make all my phone calls at once now that I'm on a roll, so I call Mila and tell her about the job.

"You haven't signed anything yet, have you?" is the first thing she asks.

I laugh, shaking my head even though she can't see that. "No Mila, you've taught me better than that. I know not to sign anything until you give me the green light."

"Good boy," she says, "very good. This is very, very good, Ian." Now I can tell she's smiling and I'm in a good mood, so I'm gonna give her a little hell.

"Wait, I'm not sure, is this a good thing?"

"You ass. I don't have time for your jokes. I've got to call ESPN and negotiate your contract."

"Thanks for not giving up on me, Mila."

"Ian, I've always known you've got that something special in you. I don't care how many times you give up on yourself, I'm not giving up on you. I know a golden ticket when I see one."

I actually burst out laughing at that. "Damn parasitic agents, always after a paycheck."

She chuckles too. "You know it."

"Okay, I've got a lot to do before this thing airs tonight, so I'll talk to you later?"

"Definitely. Keep your phone on and your wallet open. We're back in business, baby."

I roll my eyes at that, but I'm not going to argue with her. She's pumped. She's excited. Let her be. We all deserve some good news these days.

And this contract could probably fund half a dozen Turks and Caicos trips. So I can't say I blame her.

I do manage to get some more minor work done here and there, but for the most part I'm distracted, watching the clock and then watching the driveway waiting for Grant.

Finally he arrives, the promised pizza and beer in tow. We set up on the couch like we're ready for movie night and it feels kind of silly, but I also feel vindicated. I feel like I deserve this. Jack's put me through plenty and I want to watch him have to deal with just a tiny fraction of that.

Grant's curled up against me, his fingers idly teasing me through my shorts when the commercials finally end and the camera cuts to an empty table set up with microphones, surrounded by members of the press, all eagerly waiting Jack's appearance.

"What if he just didn't show up?" Grant asks suddenly. I guess he only just considered that. Which is sweet. Of course Grant expects people to follow through on what they say they'll do, because that's how Grant operates. It's naïve, but it's adorable.

"Part of me dropping my countersuit is him doing the public apology. So if he doesn't do it now, he'll have to do it later, and honestly, dragging it out is just going to make it more public. He might postpone it, but there's going to be a dozen new headlines about how he didn't show up and people that never heard about all this mess are going to suddenly care."

Grant frowns. "You really do know a lot about all this."

I shrug. "Learned the hard way. The media can be your best friend or your worst enemy. Both in the same day even. Can never be too careful."

He nudges me with his elbow, grinning now. "And you're going to be one of them, you traitor."

"Hopefully one of the good guys," I say, tightening my arm around him.

"Oh look, he actually showed," Grant says, pointing at the screen.

Jack did in fact show up, and he's not looking great. There're bags under his eyes, his face is covered in scruff, and he looks like he's been down with the flu for two weeks, but I know the truth. He's probably just been on a bender.

A man I don't recognize leans forward over the microphone and says, "Mr. Alsworth would like to read a prepared statement. There will be no questions, please."

He steps back and nods at Jack, who pulls up a piece of paper in shaky hands.

"I would like to take the opportunity to make a formal apology to anyone I have affected with the allegations I've made about my former teammate and the Hawks' management. I realize now how damaging these kinds of false claims can be and I never intended anyone any harm.

"In 2013, I was playing baseball for my college and injured myself. Due to the pain medications I received for that injury, I soon became addicted to opiates. This addiction has made me a different person than I was before, and I can see now how many people I have hurt.

"I'd like to thank everyone for their continued support as I seek treatment for my addiction and forgiveness for my past actions. And if there was ever any doubt, Ian Barrett was an entirely innocent party in all of this. He was a convenient target and nothing more. I hope I haven't done any permanent damage to his reputation."

Then, he puts the paper down, and while cameras are clicking and flashing and people are shouting questions at him, he just leaves the stage.

Grant frowns, staring at the TV in disbelief. "That's it?! *That's* his apology? After everything… He's just blaming it on drugs and not taking any responsibility!"

ASHTON CADE

I shrug. "I told you, some people are like that. Nothing's ever their fault."

"But that's not fair! He should have to... I mean... he should..."

I grin and pull him close, kissing him gently. "I love that you want to beat him up for hurting me, but it's fine. He cleared my name and that's good enough for me."

He sighs, melting into me the way he always does, the way that feels so natural and *right*. "Then it's good enough for me too."

The next few days are kind of crazy with us finalizing all our plans, picking out a place to live that's close to his office and my studio—and in a pretty great neighborhood, if I do say so myself—and finishing packing. We've done all we're going to at the camp, and it's bittersweet to leave it like this now, but I know I'll be back soon. If nothing else, there are already plans for one last barbecue Labor Day weekend before kids have to go back to school. Of course the whole Rainier family will be there. Ryan says that Troy can't wait to go swimming in the lake.

I wouldn't miss it for the world.

"You sure you're okay?" Grant asks, my truck all packed with our stuff, as I take one last look around at the camp. It's starting to look more like I remember it, but it's always going to be a part of my past. And as good as that past was, I know there's better yet to come.

For the first time in a long time, I'm looking toward the future. And in the future, I see me and Grant, building a life, maybe even starting a family. Who knows. But whatever we choose, we'll be together, and that's enough for me. That alone makes the future bright.

"With you by my side?" I ask, gripping his hand, squeezing it, my heart feeling like it's going to explode with all the love flooding it. "Absolutely."

EPILOGUE

GRANT

Labor Day Weekend

"Tell me *everything*. How's the new job? How's the apartment? Living in the city? Living with *Ian?*" May asks, waggling her eyebrows suggestively. I laugh, shaking my head.

"May, we've barely been there for a month! I don't have any of those answers for you. The job's fine, but I still don't have access to like half of the computer programs because IT hasn't gotten me into the system yet..."

She rolls her eyes. "Of course you pick the boring topic. What about Ian?"

"What about him?" I ask, my eyes wandering over to find him. He's somewhere in this crowd. It's just like the Memorial Day barbecue, only this time, everything's different. This time, I don't have to fantasize about Ian and wonder "what if." This time he's mine, and I know exactly how amazing it is to be with him, to have him in my life, to love and be loved by him.

"Give me some details! I get nothing out in this boring town."

I make a face at her. "You really want your cousin to share the intimate details of his sex life?"

May wrinkles her nose. "Not when you put it like *that*."

A sharp clap lands on my shoulder and my knees nearly buckle under the weight of Trevor's hand. "I've been looking around. You guys did a lot of work up here," he says appreciatively, nodding at the camp.

It's kind of weird to be back, I'm not going to lie. After moving to the city with Ian and starting our new lives there, the time we spent here almost doesn't feel real anymore. It feels like some kind of dream or fairytale. But the evidence is right in front of me. The spruced-up cabins, the sturdy picnic tables, the benches and the dock, it's all there, all with our fingerprints on them.

"Yeah, it wasn't all just screwing each other behind your back," I tease, even though there was basically none of that other than the very first time in the woods. That time, we were definitely sneaking around, but I'm glad that didn't go on long. I never wanted to be Ian's secret, and he didn't want to have to *have* another secret.

"Watch it," Trevor warns, glaring at me. May giggles behind her hand, trying to cover it as a cough, but Trevor's not dumb.

"I'm glad you approve. I hope we can find someone to make something out of it. It's kind of a shame it's getting abandoned again so soon," I say, looking out at the lake. I have such mixed feelings about it now. It's the place I almost died when I was a kid, but it's also the place Ian and I had our first kiss, the place where we started opening up to each other, started falling for each other.

Maybe there's something special about that lake that I never gave it credit for.

"Yeah, Ryan's going to have trouble getting Troy out of the water at this rate."

I look down to the shore and Troy and Ryan aren't the only ones in the water. There are other families splashing around and having a good time, but Ian's the only one I'm paying attention to. He's on the dock, his toes in the water.

Grabbing a couple of beers, I go down to him, sitting on the edge with him, doing everything I can to keep my nervous shaking in check.

He looks over, surprised, and takes the beer, clinking his bottle to mine.

"Feels nice to be back, doesn't it?" I ask, resting my head on his shoulder.

He shrugs. "It's not too bad, but I kind of like what we've got going for us in the city."

"Good answer." I grin.

"Incoming!"

I look up just in time to see a neon orange ball headed right for my face. I'm cringing, just waiting for the impact, but Ian reaches out with lightning-fast reflexes and catches the ball one-handed.

I'm still frozen in place when I realize my face *didn't* just get smashed by a ball.

"Nice catch," I say, not really believing he managed that, even with being a professional baseball player.

"Sorry Grant! Troy's still getting the hang of his own strength," Ryan says, wading over to us, his son bobbing along close behind with big neon floaties on his arms.

"That's okay, no harm no foul."

"Here you go," Ian says, tossing the ball back.

"Hey, I'm sorry we didn't get a chance to hang out while

you were in town," Ryan says. "Things have been crazy with the divorce and the shared custody thing…"

"I'm sorry, man. That's a bummer. I can't believe Barb cheated on you with that firefighter douchebag."

Ian gives me a look.

"What? He *is*."

Ryan grins and I can tell smiles have been rare for him lately just by the amount of effort it takes him. "You're not wrong, but I try not to talk poorly about either of them when Troy's around."

I press my lips together, eyes going wide, but Troy's off playing with some other kids now since his dad's hogging his ball.

"Sorry. Guess I'm not used to being around kids."

He sighs, shaking his head. "Not sure you ever get used to it, but it is pretty entertaining sometimes," he laughs.

Even that laugh sounds a little hollow to me. I know I don't spend a ton of time with Ryan, since he's almost ten years older than me, but he's still my cousin—practically a big brother—and seeing him hurt like this isn't okay.

"Have you been dating at all?" I ask, casually sipping on my beer.

He snorts, squeezing the foam ball, shaking his head as he looks off into the distance. "No. Not a chance. Not after what happened with Barb. That's a mess I'm going to be cleaning up for a while."

Still, despite what he says, I swear the way he looks at us is… not necessarily jealous, but… okay, kind of jealous-looking. And it could just be that he misses having a partner to spend time with at these things, that being at a family gathering kind of makes that longing worse, but I think it's something more than that. I think he sees something in our relationship in particular, which is interesting. Very interesting.

All at once, Ryan's face changes. "Troy? Troy, no, don't eat that frog!" He gives us an apologetic look before swimming off to intercept his son's snack.

"What are you thinking?" Ian asks, nudging me as I watch Ryan leave.

"Oh, nothing," I say innocently.

"Don't give me that. I know that look. I fell in love with that look. That look means trouble."

I just grin at him. "I don't know what you're talking about. I'm not the schemer in the family." I lean over and kiss him on the cheek before standing up. "I'll catch up with you later, I've got to talk to May."

"Uh-huh. I'm sure you do," he says, smirking, seeing right through me. He still doesn't try to stop me.

But that's Ian for you. He supports me unconditionally, even when he doesn't agree. I really just want to get May to promise to keep me informed of any news about Ryan, because I'm pretty sure something's up, even if he's really good at hiding it.

What can I say? Now that I've found this incredible, unbelievable happiness, I just want to spread the joy. I want everyone to be as happy as I am. As happy as Ian makes me. And who knows, maybe Ryan could be next?

ABOUT THE AUTHOR

Ashton Cade loves reading MM love stories so much, she decided to start writing her own. That way she never has to worry about running out of hot men to fantasize about. Other loves include butter tarts, cats, and anything that enhances the reading experience. Fuzzy blankets. A glass of wine. You get it.

To stay up-to-date on her latest releases, sign up for her author newsletter and be sure to follow her on Amazon.

Made in United States
Orlando, FL
25 November 2023

39391520R00146